William Henry Harrison Murray

Cones for the Camp Fire

William Henry Harrison Murray

Cones for the Camp Fire

ISBN/EAN: 9783337256623

Printed in Europe, USA, Canada, Australia, Japan

Cover: Foto ©Andreas Hilbeck / pixelio.de

More available books at **www.hansebooks.com**

CONES

FOR THE

CAMP FIRE

BY

W. H. H. (ADIRONDACK) MURRAY

— —

BOSTON
DE WOLFE, FISKE & CO.
361 AND 365 WASHINGTON ST.

DEDICATION.

To all that camp on shores of lakes, on breezy points, on banks of rivers, by sandy beaches, on slopes of mountains, and under green trees anywhere, I, an old camper, a wood lover, an aboriginal veneered with civilization, send greeting. I thank God for the multitude of you ; for the strength and beauty of you ; for the healthiness of your tastes and the naturalness of your natures. I eat and drink with you ; I hunt and fish with you ; I boat and bathe with you ; and with you by day and night enjoy the gifts of the good world. Kneeling on the deck of my yacht, stooping far over and reaching low down to fill to the brim the old camping-cup that longer than the lives of some of you has never failed my lips, and holding it high in the bright sunlight I swing it to the circle of the horizon, and standing, bare-headed, with the strong wind in my face, I drink to your health, O campers, whoever and wherever ye be. Here's health to you all and long life on the earth and something very like camping ever after.

W. H. H. MURRAY.

CONTENTS.

	PAGE
DEDICATION	3
A MOUNTAIN POOL	7
SLEEPING IN THE WOODS	9
THE BIG NEPIGON TROUT	12
A TOUGH CARRY	20
A STREAM FOR ANGLERS	24
THE GREAT GLACIER	30
A JOLLY CAMP AT RUSH LAKE	39
THE COMING OF SPRING	44
THE FOREST FIRE	46
THE BILLY GOAT	48
SHOOTING THE BUCK	52
NATURE BY DAY AND NIGHT	58
THE SONG OF THE LILY	62
THE DUEL OF THE OLD DUMB CHIEFS	65
NATURAL LAUGHTER	70
WHY THE OLD TRAPPER NEVER SMOKED	73
THE DEATH WATCH	77
ATLA'S DANCE	83
COOKING AS A GIFT	85
CHAMPLAIN'S ENTRANCE INTO THE LAKE	88

	PAGE
THE YANKEE AS A TRAVELLER. . .	92
CAMPING	95
TREES AT VANCOUVER	99
THE TRAPPER'S PARTING WITH HIS DOGS	105
SABBATH IN THE WOODS	109
THE TRAPPER'S MATCH WITH THE GAMBLER	113
HEALTHY BODIES	123
THE AMBUSH	126
MEMORY	139
THE TRAPPER'S IDEA OF THE HERE-AFTER	142
GAMBLER'S DEATH	148
THE GREAT NATIONAL PARK . . .	167
L'ENVOY	187

CONES FOR THE CAMP-FIRE.

A MOUNTAIN POOL.

OW beautiful is a pool among the mountains! Small as it may be, how it can collect and reflect the great world above and around it! It may not be as big as a cliff, and yet a hundred cliffs are in it. A single pine may bridge it, nevertheless it accommodates miles upon miles of forest. Small as it is, the great sun comes and bathes in its depth. Acres of clouds float through it. The sky, the numberless hills with all their countless trees, the mountains so vast, their innumerable peaks, — within its scant space all are grouped and

none are crowded. Sweet miracle
of the woods, placid mirror of the
hills and skies, gentle eye of the
forest upon whose clear retina is
focused the sublimities of heaven
and the beauties of surrounding
earth, how often hast thou lost me
game and sport because thy loveliness held me pensive at thy grassy
rim ! — *From " Daylight Land."*

MAGINE your bed-chamber of odorous bark, and your bed of pungent boughs. Your couch made under murmuring trees and within a few yards of the lazily moving water, whose motions caress rather than chafe the shore. Stretched your full length on such a couch, spread in such a place, the process of falling asleep becomes an experience. You lie and watch yourself to observe the gradual departure of your senses. Little by little you feel yourself passing away. Slowly and easily as an ebbing tide you begin to pass into the dim and insensible realm beyond the line of feeling. At last a moment comes in which you know

you are passing over the very
verge of consciousness. You are
aware that you are about to fall
asleep. Your cheek but partially
interprets the cool pressure of the
night wind; your ears drowsily
surrender the lingering murmur
of beach and pine; your eyes
droop their lids little by little;
your nose slightly senses the odor
of the piny air, as you mechanically draw it in; the chest falls as
it passes as mechanically out, and
then — you are asleep.

The hours pass, and still you
sleep on. The body, in obedience
to some occult law of force within
the insensible frame, still keeps up
its respirations; but you are some-
where — sleeping. At last the
pine above you, in the deep hush
which precedes the coming of
dawn, stills its monotone, and
silence weaves its airy web amid
the motionless stems. The water
falls asleep. The loon's head is
under its spotted wing, and the

owl becomes mute.   The deer has
left the shore, and lies curved in
its mossy bed.   The rats no longer
draw their tiny wake across the
creek, and the frogs have ceased
their croaking.   All is quiet.   In
the profound quiet, and unconscious of it all, the sleeper sleeps.
What sleep such sleeping is ! and
what a ministry is being ministered
unto mind and body through the
cool, pure air, pungent with gummy
odors, and strong with the smell of
the sod and the root-laced mould
of the underlying earth ! — *From
"Lake Champlain and its Shores."*

THE BIG NEPIGON TROUT.

S I spoke, the train struck the bridge which stretches across the noble and noted river, and as it was gliding smoothly on it slowed, and suddenly stopped

"Oh! oh! oh!"

"See, Tom! Look!"

"Jones, where are you?"

"Fo' de Lawd, Mars' Judge!" exclaimed the waiter. "You two gem'men git to de hind end ob de kyar, ef you wants ter see what's gwine on down dar in dat ribber!"

The excitement was contagious, for the car was full of shouts, cheers, and exclamations. The Judge rushed down the aisle to the rear of the car, —

"Great heavens!" he exclaimed,

as he reached the platform.
"Look at that!"

A hundred feet below us flowed
the noble current, a deep, wide,
strong-moving mass of water.
Here and there an eddy marked
it with its huge circumference.
But in the main it moved downward toward the great lake, shining in full view, as a river flows
between widened banks and with
plenty of room. In the middle of
the river nearly under us was a
canoe with an Indian at either end,
and a man in a velveteen jacket
standing in the centre. In his
hands was a rod, and the tip of the
rod was doubled backward nigh to
the reel, the ringing whir of which
filled the air. His pose was that
of an angler who had struck a fish
— a big fish, a fish that is fighting
him gamely and stubbornly, and
which he is resisting with the cool,
determined skill of a veteran of
the rod.

"What a picture!" exclaimed

the Judge. "Gad! what a picture!"

Well might he exclaim, "What a picture!" The wide river; the island-studded lake, into which it emptied; the lofty banks; the great dome of blue sky above; high over the stream, as if hung in mid-air, the long train, every window filled with heads, every platform crowded with forms, the engineer, an angler himself, hanging out of the cab, swinging his hat; below, the canoe, the ochred Indians, the bent body of the angler, the swaying, quivering, doubled-up rod, — what a picture!

Suddenly, we who were looking saw the rod straighten. Some of us knew what it meant. The Judge clinched my arm, and in an instant out of the water came the trout, mouth open, fins extended, tail spread.

"Jerusalem!" screamed the Judge. "He's a twenty-pounder!"

Dear old Judge, thou hadst the

true angler's eye — that eye which enlarges and multiplies by a happy trick of vision, not merely the size of the fish, but the enjoyment of the soul. Ay, ay, it was a twenty-pounder to both of us old sports for the instant, and if the envious scales did shrink the noble form to shorter and thinner proportions, it could not rob us of the ecstasy of our first estimate, thank heaven!

And the fight that followed — what words may set it forth? O anglers, shut your eyes, and see and hear it from behind your closed lids. Call memory to your aid — the memory of the sternest fight you ever fought, of the swiftest torrent, of the wildest pool, of that favorite rod smashed to splinters, of paddle broken, of the " biggest fish that ever swam " lost or won. Stop, I say, and from behind closed lids see all this, and you will see what we saw under the great bridge over the Nepigon on that bright June day.

Whoever the Man in the Velveteen Jacket might be, he was of the right sort, an angler of whom anglers need never be ashamed; for as he fought that fish he gave us such an exhibition of angler's fence as ranked him one of the best that ever fingered reel. An eight-ounce rod against an eight-pound fish, a strong, deep current, and a Nepigon canoe: grant anglers such conditions, and how many shall make a winning fight?

Twice the huge fish broke water, and twice the long train cheered him to the echo. The Judge was wild. Each time the fish broke the surface, he fairly jumped. He leaned far over the rail. He swung his hat, and when the monstrous trout broke the surface the second time, he yelled, —

"Save him, save him, and I'll nominate you for the Presidency!"

Once the great fish for an instant burst through his opponent's

guard. Once, I must confess, my
heart sank within me, as a stone
sinks to the bottom of a well.
When he was a hundred feet from
the canoe, the rod nearly tip and
butt, and the silk line stretched
through the air like a wire, the fish
doubled and lanced backward like
a flash. We saw his wake, — that
sharpened wedge of water which
anglers dread, — and as he went
under the canoe, and in the stillness that had come to us we heard
the line rattle on the bark, a groan
escaped the Judge. He rolled his
eyes upward, and roared as if
stricken with pain, —

"Great Scott! he's lost him!"

But the fish was not lost. The
angler recovered his advantage,
and fought the fight to the end,
skilfully and coolly. The fish was
deftly gaffed by one of . the
Indians, and quickly lay on the
bottom of the canoe. The
Indians seized their paddles, and
the light craft glanced toward the

western bank, the man unjointing
his rod as the boat shot along, and
in a moment they came panting
up the embankment with a huge
hamper in their hands, in which,
amid flowers and grasses, lay six
other trout, nearly as large as the
one we had seen captured.

Seldom is such a reception
granted to a mortal as was given
to the Man in the Velveteen
Jacket.   The engineer cheered and
swung his hat ; the fireman, sooted
and begrimed, capered and danced
on the coal-box like an electrified
imp; the passengers yelled ; the
ladies fluttered their handkerchiefs ;
while we anglers of the party
fairly took him in our arms and
lifted him on to the platform,
where the Judge infolded him in
an embrace which the stranger
will never forget, — a hug such as
an old angler gives a younger one
to whom he is indebted for an exhibition of skill which has brought
back to his memory all his own

former victories, and proved to his anxious soul that the gentle art is not being neglected.

Never fear, never fear, dear old Judge, that the art of all arts will be lost, or the skill of trained finger and eye be forgotten. We shall pass; but still the streams will flow on, the pools will go round, and the trout love the coolness of springs and the rush of swift waters. The boys will grow up like their sires, loving water and sun, loving forest and rapids. With brown faces and hands, and with eyes keen as ours, they will stand where we stood, they will boat where we boated, they will camp where we camped, and the dead ashes of fires that we kindled they will kindle to new life again. The gentle art will live on, while nature is nature, and mankind is man. — *From "Daylight Land."*

A TOUGH CARRY.

OME, Henry, let us halt a minit and git breath. This is sartinly a tough carry, and ye be loaded like a sinner at the Day of Jedg-ment, when, as I have heerd the missioners say, mortals will be summoned into court with all their divilments on top of 'em. And while ye have nothin' that an honest man need be ashamed of, even in front of the Lord, yet I will say that ye be mightily heavily cumbered with the fixin's, for sartin, and yer legs must feel in a rebellious state agin sech treat-ment as ye've been givin' 'em for the last mile; for ef there's any-thing that will set the siners in a man's thighs twitchin' and sort of

knottin'-up like, it's fetchin a carry
through a tamarack swamp like
this, with a whole camp on his
back, and no bottom wuth speakin'
on under ye. That's right, — set-
tle down there on that bog and
squirm out of the straps and ease
yerself a while. I'll bet that the
wales on yer shoulders be red as a
rat's hide when the meat has peeled
with it; and as for yer neck, the
infarnal basket, Henry, has rasped
it like a file. How do ye feel inwardly, for I know ye smart out-
wardly?"

"Oh, I feel all right," replied
his companion. "Of course the
straps have cut into me a little,
and the basket has worn through
the cuticle somewhat, I guess, by
the feeling on my neck; but I am
good for the distance between here
and the lake, wherever it is; and
when we get through, if it is a
decent place to look at, we will
take a rest and a good strong meal
too, for I am as empty as a last
year's gourd."

"I like the sound of yer talk, Henry," said the old man, whom our readers will have easily recog- nized as John Norton, the Trapper, and his companion as Henry Her- bert. "I like the sound of yer talk," continued the old man, laugh- ing ; "and I can well believe ye ; for ye have the look of a man whose loadin' is all on the outside and none of it in, and I should ventur' the opinion that a pound or two of that steak ye have in the basket there, jediciously spitted and eaten slowly, 'twixt proper allowances of corn cakes and spring water, rein- forced with a few leaves of the tea, would round ye out and make ye look sort of inhabited-like ; for I have always noted that a man with no vict'als in him looks like a de- sarted settlement, — kinder lone- some, and a good deal as ef a funeral was goin' on inside of him. But another good lift will bring us out of this snarl of tamarack and put our feet onto the beach of as

handsome a lake as the Lord ever
made, even here in these woods,
where He does seem to have did
His best, and kept at it a long
while, too ; for I think, 'twixt trap-
pin' and boatin', I've been on a
thousand of 'em off and on in the
last forty year ; but a prittier one
than lies ahead of us never had its
springs set runnin', ef I am any
jedge. So crawl into yer straps,
Henry, and I will give yer pack a
h'ist, and we will see how soon we
can fetch out of this divilment of
bushes ; for a tamarack swamp is
the divil's own work in natur' for
sartin ; and ef a man who be
nothin' but ordinary, and hasn't
been favored in pious edication,
can bring a boat or a pack through
one of 'em and not get sort of strong
and 'arnest like in his speech, it be
because the Lord is onusually marciful to him while he is at it." —
*From " The Story of the Man who
didn't know much." Adirondack
Tales.*

A STREAM FOR ANGLERS.

 KNOW a stream among the hills, which glides down steep declines, flows across level stretches and tumbles over rocky verges into dark ravines. Over it are white birches, and firs, and fragrant cedars, some spruces, tall and straight, and here and there an oak or mountain ash. The breezes, born of cool currents that pour downward from upper heights, where snow whitens yet, blow along this stream among the mountains full of ozone, brewed in the upper atmospheres, and which the nose of the climber drinks as the Homeric gods drank their wine, leisurely, because it is so strong and pure. In the spruces along this stream live two big, brown owls

that doze through the day, and if
you will sit for an hour and listen
you will hear them mutter and
murmur in their dreams; dreaming
of mice in the meadow, and young
chickens in the lowlands, I fancy.
On the largest oak, old and gnarled,
at the end of a dead bough, a
white-headed eagle sits watchfully.
Twenty feet below him his mate is
hovering over four eggs in a huge
nest made of dry sticks. Their
eyes have seen more suns rise and
set than mine, and will see the
crimson long after mine are closed
forever, doubtless. All men are
their foes, yet they live on. All
men are my friends, still I must
die. Queer, isn't it?

There are anglers on this mountain stream, but only I know them.
They fish each day, and each day
fill their creels, and yet they use
no rods, nor lines, nor hooks, nor
flies, nor bait. It is because I have
never fished this hidden stream
myself that I have seen them fish

it. Poachers? Nay. This brook
is their preserve, and I would be a
poacher on their rights should I
cast line across it. Who are these
strange anglers that angle so
strangely?

The oldest of them is a snapping
turtle, and a great angler he is in
truth. I ambushed him as he lay
asleep on a log one day, and on
his back was written, A.D. 1710.
That makes him one hundred and
eighty years old — an age that all
good anglers ought to live to. Do
you tell me " That was a lie ; he
couldn't be so old?" It may be
so — I won't quarrel with you,
friend. Regard it as a bit of his-
tory, and I will agree with you.
But he is a great angler, this old
turtle, and has caught more trout
than any angler who reads this
passage — ten to one, I warrant.

The best angler of them all —
better than the water-snake or the
kingfisher, or the mountain cat, or
the turtle, wise as he is — is an

old brown mink. He is so old that
his face is gray and his fur shabby,
but he is a wise old angler. Six
days I watched him come to the
stream, and six good half-pound
trout did I see the old gray veteran
sit and eat on the cool, damp ledge
against which the whirling bubbles
ran. It was a sight to see him
wash himself after his repast! And
after he had thoroughly washed
his mouth and cleansed his hands,
he would stand and look into the
deep, dark pool for a moment, con-
templatively, as I fancied. Perhaps
the old fellow was saying his grace.
Perhaps he is a deacon among the
minks! Who knows? Isn't a good
angler as good as a deacon, any-
way?

There is a bit of meadow on the
stream enclosed with a fringe of
white birches and cedar growths;
and amid the green grasses of it
are cranberry vines, and bunches
of beaver cups; white and blue
flowers speck it with color, and the

earth odors are strong over it. It is
pleasant to stand in it and breathe
in the aboriginal scents of wild roots
and uncultivated mould. The un-
tameable in me fraternizes so lovingly with this rare bit of untamed
nature. This little mountain meadow, from whose stretch the beaver,
with their sharp teeth, cut the trees
centuries ago, is so real and genuine that it charges its influence to
the very core of me. It is so natural that it makes me more so.   •

The old beaver dam is still there,
and over it the water pours with
soft noises into a deep and wide
pool. On one side of this dark bit
of water is a great rock. Its front
is covered with thick mosses very
rich in color. Across it wanders a
vine with little red berries strung
on it. Can you see the old beaver
dam, the pool, the big rock, the
moss, the running vine and the
shining red berries? Yes? Very
likely you can; but, oh, you who
have such eyes to see — you cannot

see the huge trout whose home that
dark, deep pool is, and which I have
seen so many times as he rose for
the bug or grub that I tossed him.
And once as I lay on the edge of
the pool, hidden in the long grasses,
I saw him at play, having a frolic
all by himself, and, oh, he made
that space of gloomy water irides-
cent as he flashed and flew through
it. Where is he? Do you really
wish to know? Well, I will be good
and tell you. He is where I found
him.

THE GREAT GLACIER.

O we stood steadfastly gazing at the vast vision, enraptured, when an exclamation from a man behind us faced us around, and there, to the north and east, we saw a sight which may not, perhaps, be matched in its grandeur and surroundings on this earth of ours. A glacier, vast, lofty, immense, buttressed, fissured, creviced, — a section of the Mississippi tilted up obliquely and frozen solid; the St. Lawrence pouring bodily over a mountain range ten thousand feet above you and turned on the instant into ice, stiffened solid at its maddest plunge; a creation of ten thousand years; a monument above those past, dead years, which all

the rain and shine of other equal
years to come will not efface;
standing cold, monstrous, motionless, silent, sublime, within a distance so short from our parlor car
that even the weakest woman or
smallest child in it might, by an
easy stroll, stand under its ponder-
ous front. Heavens! how small,
how feeble, how insignificant
seemed the engine of our heavy
train, with its sobs, and pantings,
and puny puffs of power, beside
that monstrous creation of ages,
that landscape of frozen force, that
overhanging world of chained
energy which, should Nature ever
loosen the chilled links that
chained it to that mountain pass,
would sweep our engine, train, and
yonder house away like chips; ay,
crush, grind and pulverize them all
to finest dust, so fine that, were it
dry, the winds might lift it as they
lift ashes, and blow it through the
air, invisible to mortal eye.

"Never shall it be said," exclaimed the Judge, "that I came to such an environment of majesty as this and passed heedlessly on. Here we will stop a day and a night, and see the sunset splendor and the sunrise glory on these peaks, and the moonlight whiten the surface of that frozen field. There is not ice enough in Switzerland to make that single glacier yonder. Let the train move on. We four have wandered on the earth too widely and seen too many of its wonders not to recognize the extraordinary and do homage to it."

And so the train rolled down the grade, around the swell of the mountain beyond, and left us four gray-headed boys standing above the glacial torrent, gazing and wondering.

That afternoon we took the trail — an easy way, which led us to the Glacier's front. Slowly we drew our line of progress toward it. The fit mood was on us all. We were alone, we four. We were intelligent enough to appreciate the awful phenomenon. We saw it with the eyes of many years. We could measure it by European comparison. We could weigh it in the scales of world-wide knowledge. Two of us had footed the Alpine passes. One had seen the Himalayas. Another had wintered within the Arctic Circle.

Slowly we moved forward. A few rods of motion onward, and we would pause. We were all eyes, all feeling. We felt we were approaching a fragment of eternity. We were drawing nigh to, and gazing at, a bit of the everlasting. Before us was the work of ages. Here the centuries had stopped. Between these monstrous mountains Time had come to a full halt, powerless to go one foot farther. Here before us, with folded wings, white-faced, hoary-headed, his scythe held in his stiffened hands, we saw him stand, a statue of ice.

"Older than Rome, older than Egypt, older than Man!" murmured the Judge solemnly, as he gazed.

In front of the Glacier was a great round wall of sand, of cobbles, of bowlders. Its pressure drove downward to the bed rock of the world, and ploughed the surface earth.

"This plough ploughs slowly, but it ploughs deep," remarked Colonel Goffe, as he ran his eye along the huge ridge.

"Think who steadies it!" said the Judge.

The sun sank from sight behind the western ridge. The gray shaft of Sir Donald flushed, reddened, then blazed as with fire.

From amid the dark firs above us Night softly shook her raven plumage, and feathered us with gloom. Then she spread her sable wings. She soared upward, and the world darkened. Anon she sailed, a vast formation of blackness above the peaks. The skies saw her coming, and welcomed her with every window lighted. The Indian myth was realized. The Raven brooded the world.

But the great Glacier amid the gloom still showed whitely. From between the pillars of darkness, from the cavernous blackness of night, it looked forth like the face of a dead man from the mouth of a grave.

"Older than Night, and hence stronger!" whispered the Judge.

Thus we four sat in the darkness watching and pondering, while through the gloom and the stillness the glacial torrent at our feet tore its line of hoarse noise.

"See!" I exclaimed. "The Glacier is growing whiter. Its paleness begins to brighten. Look! There is a gleam in that upper crevice! And see — see that flash of white!"

"The moon! The moon!" cried the Judge. "The moon is rising.

Now we shall see the spectacle of
a lifetime ! "

Excuse me, reader, I cannot
write it down.. I know the limita-
tion of letters. Even could I tint
them with all the colors of the
palette, it were in vain. Imagine
our position, standing in that
gorge, deep, deep down at the very
roots of those monstrous mountains, within the enclosure of their
awful environment ; the stillness
which the roar of the torrent
divided, but did not disturb; the
whole world black with the blackness of night when it smothers the
woods out of sight of the eye ; the
great Glacier in front of us, vast,
monstrous, formless, as it lay dimly
outlined in the gloom ; then
imagine it growing, growing, growing upon the sight. See it brighten
and widen out into view.

See the gleams begin to run
over it. See that flash of white
fire strike the crest and run crink-
ling along the lofty ridge until it

connects the two opposite peaks
with a line of living light.

See the crevices gleam and
glisten brighter and brighter. Behold the sparkles and flashes of
fire start up here and there, at
random, flash, shift and fade, and
then, as the rounded orb, vast of
size, intense, rose majestically
above the summit and looked
calmly, and, as it seemed, admir-
ingly down upon it, behold, in
your imagination, what we saw, —
the monstrous mountains darkly
forested round about us, between
which, wide as a landscape, lay
the great Glacier, bathed in soft
white radiance from side to side,
from base to summit, and above
it the dome of the sky, and
suspended from it the round
moon !

"Day unto day uttereth speech,
and night unto night showeth
knowledge," said the Judge rever-
ently, and we turned slowly from
the sublime spectacle before us,

and started to pick our way carefully down the trail.

We had seen the Glacier!   It
was   enough. — *From   "Daylight
Land."*

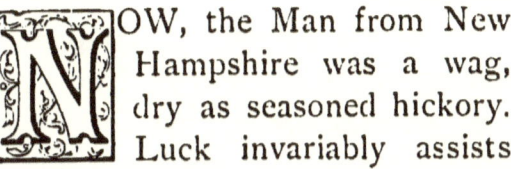OW, the Man from New Hampshire was a wag, dry as seasoned hickory. Luck invariably assists such a man when bent on a joke, and luck had assisted this gray-headed joker to such an armament as many readers of this book, I am sure, never saw. In a gun-shop at Winnipeg he had found an old-fashioned flintlock, known among our forefathers as a king's arm. It was of monstrous bore, thick at the breech and thin at the muzzle; with a strong stock mounted heavily in solid brass, and an iron ramrod. The flint was half the size of a small fire-shovel, while the pan was as large as an iron spoon. It was a venerable relic

of former days and men; a murderous old gun, if you had shot
and powder enough to charge it
properly, and you could ever get it
off; but most eccentric and unre-
liable in its habits. The gun was
apparently strong as ever, and as
to its barrel, in good repair; but
the lock was lashed to its place by
stout leather thongs, and unless
the powder was coarse, the grains
would leak through between the
barrel and the pan into the recess
where the springs and tumbler
were located. The spectacle which
the Colonel presented when he
stood equipped for the day, — a big
powder-horn with a wooden stopple
under his elbow, one pocket sag-
ging with shot, the other stuffed
full of oakum and paper for his
wadding, the old gun in his hand,
and a white bell-crowned hat on
his head, which he had found by
the same luck that got him his
gun, was of so funny a sort that
the camp roared with laughter.

But the Colonel took the jokes that we fired at him with imperturbable gravity, and we knew that if ever he did get that old gun off, and there were any ducks in the landscape within range, the Indian encampment would be fed full to feasting.

In less than an hour each of us had his bag except the Colonel. " For some unexplainable reason," as he stated, he had been " unable to get the old thing off." But he assured us he had confidence in his piece, and that sooner or later the world would hear from him. There was not one of us that did not admire both his courage and perseverance, for he stood bravely up behind the old mortar, and pulled the trigger at every duck that came by.

" Lord!" said the Judge, " what would become of the Colonel if the old thing should go off ? " So we patiently trailed in the rear of his canoe in response to the Colonel's

exhortation, "to stand by the insti-
tution of the fathers." Advice
and interrogations were rained
upon him. The Judge wanted to
know "if he had loaded every time
he snapped, and if he knew how
many charges there were in the
piece?" Mr. Pepperell inquired
"if he had powder enough to keep
on priming for the rest of the
day?" And Osgood suggested
that we each "take our turn and
spell him at pulling the trigger."

Meanwhile, as we had stopped
shooting, the ducks had settled
thicker and thicker, till the water
was black and the sedge was full
of feathers, and the Colonel worked
away at the ancient bit of machinery
with redoubled vigor. He who
says that the age of miracles has
passed is an idiot, for that old gun
finally went off — went off at an
opportune moment, too, for the
canoe was wedged into the sedge,
the Colonel well braced, and the
air filled with ducks. Granted the

air black with birds ; an old king's arm charged with a gill or more of coarse shot, and a man from New Hampshire squinting grimly over the breech-pin, and there could be but one result, or, rather, three results. The gun jumped out of his hands, the Colonel sat down in the boat with a crash, and ducks fell by the dozen. It was a monstrous bag in truth, and the Colonel took the honors of the day and week ; for while he averaged less than five shots a day, still the totals beat every gun in the crowd. One thing is sure, the Indians who camped with us on Rush Lake that week will never forget that old flintlock gun or the Man from New Hampshire, nor shall we who were there ever forget the sport and the fun.—*From " Daylight Land."*

THE COMING OF SPRING.

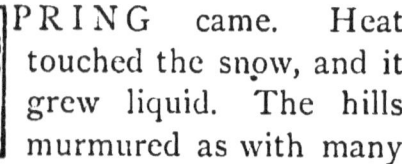PRING came. Heat touched the snow, and it grew liquid. The hills murmured as with many tongues, and low music flowed rippling down their sides. The warm earth sweetened with odors. Sap stirred in root and bough, and the fibred sod thrilled with delicious passages of new life.

From the far South came flaming plumage, breasts of gold and winged music to the groves. The pent roots of herbs, spiced and pungent, burst upward through the moistened mould, and breathed wild, gamy odors through the woods. The skeleton trees thickened with leaf formations, and hid their naked grayness under green

and gold. Each day birds of passage, pressed by parental instinct,
slanted wings toward the lake, and,
sailing inward to secluded bays,
made haste to search for nests.
Mother otters swam heavy through
the tide, and the great turtles,
lumbering from the water, digged
deep pits under starlight, in the
sand, and cunningly piled their
pyramid of eggs. All nature loved
and mated, each class of life in its
own order, and God began the
recreation of the world. — *From
" Mamelons."*

THE FOREST FIRE.

HE fire was that old one which burnt itself into the memories of men so it became a birthmark, and thus was handed down to generations. None knew how kindled. It first flared westward of the shallow lake, where Mistassinni empties its brown waters from the north, and at the first flash flamed to the sky. It is a mystery to this day, for never did fire kindled in woods or grass run as it ran. It raced a race of death with every living thing ahead of it, and won against the swiftest foot of man or moose. The whirring partridge, buzzing on for life, tumbled, featherless, a lump of singed, palpitating flesh, into the ashes.

The eagle, circling a mile from
earth, caught in the rising vortex
of hot air, shrunk like a feather
touched by heat, and, lessening as
he dropped, reached earth a cinder.
The living were cremated as they
crouched in terror or fled scream-
ing. The woods were hot as hell.
Trees, wet mosses, sodden mould,
brooks, springs, and even rivers
disappeared. Rocks cracked like
cannon overcharged. The face
of cliffs slid downward or fell off
with crashes like split thunder.
It was a fire as hot, as fierce, as
those persistent flames which melt
the solid core of the world.

— *From " Mamelons."*

THE BILLY GOAT.

OW, as you know, gentle-
men, there is a good deal
of 'dynamite' in a billy
goat. It won't do to drop
on to one suddenly, unless you wish
to be lifted. Any man who runs
against a goat suddenly, without
telegraphing him beforehand, acts
as if his business education had
been neglected. For a goat is the
embodiment of a terrific energy
when aroused, and nothing starts
him quicker than a sudden appearance. Any man who approaches
him without circumspection is liable to lose some part of himself,
as it were. More than one man
has lost his balance and his self-
respect by such carelessness. Both
these essentials of standing and

character are apt to remain absent during the entire interview.

"A goat is endowed with great quickness of apprehension, and he acts on his impulses. When a goat of the masculine gender stands and gazes at you with a look of curious deliberation in his eyes, you will, if you are a rational being, promptly pick the nearest tree and get behind it. This is the only wise course to adopt. Nor should you be slow in doing this. It is not safe to take any chances with a billy goat if he is within fifty feet of you and has in his own mind decided to act. You cannot rely on his remaining where he is any considerable length of time. He is apt to move suddenly, and when he moves he always moves in a straight line, and with his objective point clearly in view.

"To know a goat thoroughly, gentlemen, I am convinced that a man should begin his investigations in childhood. The knowledge

needed is not acquired readily by
an adult. A man can pilot a
steamboat better than a boy, but
to steer a goat successfully into a
paddock without any back action
of the paddles is a feat at which a
boy will beat his father every time.
The innocent sprightliness of early
life is an essential element of success in such an undertaking. A
deacon of mature age and dignity
of character might do it, but he
would never be fit to hold his office
after he had finished the job. His
record would be broken, as it were.
What he had gained in fluency of
expression he would have lost in
resignation of spirit and the sweet
placidness of his vocabulary. A
deacon should always leave the
management of a billy goat to his
hired boy, and keep out of hearing
when the boy and the goat are in
close communication, too. Any
material departure from this rule
will always result in unhappiness.
The manners of the goat will be

spoiled, and the deacon — if the matter be fully reported — will surely lose his office.

"A goat is like any other highly organized creation. He learns evil fast and forgets it slowly. He is a creature of vanity, and relishes success. After he has learned a man's anatomy by experiment, the knowledge is fixed in his mind forever. Time may obliterate the impression he has made on you, but it never obliterates the impression you have made on him. Years may pass ; your hairs may be whiter and his coarser, but if he ever gets a chance to hit you again, your years and venerable appearance will not save you. The old reprobate will hit you in the same spot. I have never been able to satisfactorily explain this to my own mind, but the fact remains. I have seen it demonstrated." — *From "Daylight Land."*

SHOOTING THE BUCK.

S the Trapper concluded his speech the canoe began to move toward the buck, but with a motion so easy and true to the line of its progress that, to one looking at it in the direction of its movement, the movement itself could not be perceived. The arms of the Trapper were sunk well over the sides of the canoe, and his paddle played in the water, without revealing its motions, as noise-lessly and almost as invisibly as do the webbed feet of the Northern Diver. His body was so held as to place Herbert's form exactly between the buck and himself, so that neither the motion of the canoe, as it slowly floated forward, nor the body and motions of the paddler, could be seen. Herbert sat in plain view, with his rifle across his knees, and his finger within the guard ; but his body was as motionless as if carved out of the air, and the features of his face, even, were stiffened into the rigidity of marble. Thus the canoe glided into the deepening shadows of the western shore and the mouth of the little cove, directly toward the game.

At the farther end of the bay stood the buck, his feet deep in the brown sands, and his antlered head lifted, as if in proud challenge, into the air. His posture was one of haughty interrogation as to what the dim object gliding in upon him might be, and superb defiance of it. Twice he lifted a foreleg and drove his pointed hoof into the sand, with the expression of lordly impatience at the ignorance or audacity of those who dared disturb, by their bold presence, his

royal privacy. And as .the canoe
floated still nearer, twice he lifted
his brown muzzle and blew a blast
from his resounding nostrils that
tore fiercely through the still air,
and made the woods behind him
ring again, while the mountain
across the lake received the wrathful sound, and passed it 'back in
diminutive modulations to the spot
whence it came. Once he started,
as if some terrible suspicion had
for an instant broken over the
ramparts of his courage and
stormed into the very pavilion of
his kingly spirit ; but it was only
a passing weakness. He gave one
jump ; then stopped, planted himself as if incapable of fear ; lifted
his nose high up, and blew again
a wrathful challenge to the rude
intruders, while the hair on the
line of his back ridged in wrath,
and his feet smote the beach like
hammers.

In the mean while the canoe
floated as noiselessly onward as a

feather, and with a steadiness of motion that never varied a hair's width. Even when the buck jumped, not a muscle of Herbert's face moved, and the finger which lay lightly on the trigger could not have been steadier had the hand to which it belonged been incapable of feeling. Thus the man in the bow held his position with rigid fixedness, and the man in the stern worked his paddle with the same even and steady play of the wrist. But when the buck blew his second challenge, after he made his bound, and the progress of the canoe was fast bringing his head in line with a beech, whose silvery-white leaves furnished a background that would serve to bring out his head in partial relief at least, the paddle of the Trapper stopped its movement, and settled to a trail, and when the onward progress had lifted the antlers to the level of the silver leaves, the least possible quiver ran along the sides of the canoe.

For a second after the signal was given, Herbert moved not a muscle, and then the rifle jumped to his cheek, and before it would seem possible for his eye to have found the line of the sight, the fiery flame leapt into the dusky air, and the mountains rang with the rattling echoes of the sharp explosion. The buck never jumped, but dropped in his tracks as if his legs had been cut from under him, and lay in a limp heap; for the bullet had entered between the eyes and torn its passage through the spinal column as it passed out. The Trapper said not a word until he had reached the spot where the dead deer lay, and had examined both the entrance and exit of the bullet; but after he had bled the game, and had wiped his knife free of stain, he turned to his comrade, and said, —

"I knowed ye could shoot well

afore to-day, for I've seed ye do
shootin' that would put to shame
many who boast of their exploits
with the rifle ; but what ye have
done here on the buck shows the
parfection of the weepon ye carry,
and that yer gifts lie in the direction of a grooved barrel. I sartinly thought ye was waitin' a
leetle too long on the cretur arter
I gin ye the signal, and my in'ards
sort of shrivelled with disapp'int-
ment at the idee of losing him,
but I conceit the reason of yer
waitin' now I've seed where ye've
drove the bullit, and I confess ye
mixed yer brains with yer powder
and shot with reason and jedgment, for the body showed dim
agin the bank, and the white leaves
of the beech here made his head
yer best chance ; but the chance
was none of the best, and I hon-
estly question ef there's another
man in the woods that could have
did as ye have done considerin'
the darkness and the distance." —
From "Adirondack Tales." Vol. i.

NATURE BY DAY AND NIGHT.

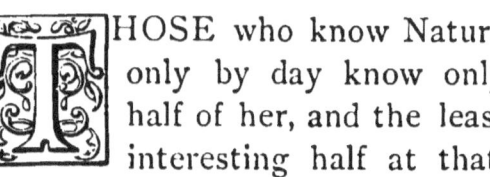HOSE who know Nature only by day know only half of her, and the least interesting half at that. Nature has two faces. Both are beautiful, but one is supremely so. The one is as a human face, glowing, sunlighted, tanned, scarred, it may be, perfect or imperfect, as the day is. Her night-time face is as an angel's, the face of one that has been translated from flesh to spirit, and by the translation lost its grossness and become etherealized. Its beauty is that beauty which is veiled, which gains from having its loveliness suggested rather than revealed. The nude is always unsatisfactory, for loveliness is ever a thing of suggestion rather than

revelation. He who sees all plainly sees too much. As sight would rob religion of the glory of faith, so it robs loveliness of the benefits of imagination.

One may tire of Nature by day, —the sun makes her common. When morning has fully come, we may go within-doors and eat ; we may go to our toil ; we may strike our tents and move on, weary of the dusty road. For not until the glare is passed, and the hot sun dimmed by coming shadows and cooled by falling dew, need we halt on the march or come forth from our doors to look about us. Verily to the lover of Nature, whether on plain or amid hills, or shore of sea, the night is the time to wake. Then should eyes be opened as stars and orbed for vision, as is the moon when it rolls in rounded perfection through the lighted skies.

And oh, the voices of the night ! The day is tuneless. Man monopolizes it with his noises ; with the

murmurs of his trade, the roar and
rumble of his commerce ; with the
strident calls of his shoutings, his
cursing, and his turbulence. But
with the night comes that silence
which is vocal. Then Nature sings.
Her tunefulness is heard abroad,
and her soft melodies come sweetly
to listening ears. The sod finds
speech ; the brook murmurs to the
banks ; the trees whisper and call
in sylvan concert ; and through all
the fields a thousand tongues, unknown among the languages of
men, break forth in sweet expression.

To many I know that what I
write will be a mystery, or only as
the joining of meaningless words,
but to others it will come freighted
with soberness and truth. For
they, as well as I, have camped
upon the shores of lakes amid the
circling woods ; have stood alone
at night on boundless prairies, and
thrown themselves down amid the
grasses and flowers, unable to sleep

because of the glory that was above
them, the odors that they breathed,
and the sweet sounds which came
to their charmed ears from nigh or
far. And others yet have stood
upon the top of mountains when
the sun went down, and with glad-
ness seen the shadows darken and
the stars come out, watching for
them as for loved faces not seen
for years, and have sat on the bare
rocks, hour after hour, and watched
them draw their golden circles
through the blue above, and in the
silence heard all the tones of memory and the prophecies of hope.
And when at last they slept, they
found the granite softer than a
downy bed shut in with walls and
doors. These, reading, know what
I mean, and that I say the truth
and lie not, when I say, that he who
has seen Nature only by day has
seen only the lesser half of her,
and in one sense, and a true one
too, has not seen her at all. — *From
"Daylight Land."*

THE SONG OF THE LILY.

I.

AVE you breathed me by night,
  when on the still air
Came the song of the lute, came
  the murmur of prayer?
Have you breathed me at morn,
  when the odorous trees
Were thrilled from their sleep by the kiss
  of the breeze?
Have you breathed me when mingled with
  mine was the breath
Of the woman you loved, and must love till
  death,
As her lips clung to yours their caress to
  bestow,
While I lifted and sank on her bosom of
  snow?
If you have, then you know that no other
  such bloom
Blooms for man or for woman 'twixt cradle
  and tomb.

II.

Oh, for love and for lovers my perfume is
  shed.
I am flower of the living, I am flower of the
  dead.

At the feasts of the rich, by the lovely and fair,
I am grouped in the cups, I am twined in
the hair.
By the hand of the groom, ere he sleeps by
her side,
My white leaves are sown on the couch of
the bride.
And if she be taken, on the door of her
tomb,
As a sign and a symbol, he chisels my bloom.
Oh, for love and for lovers, not since the
sweet air
Has been breathed with their sighs has there
been flower so fair.

III.

I am old as the world. When the Stars of
the morn
Sang together for joy, for their joy I was
born.
In the dawn of the world, when women
were given   ′
In their sweetness to men, I was dropped
down from heaven,
To be charm for their charms, and a potion,
for never
Did a lover love once, and not love forever,
The woman that wore me on her bosom the
night
When he knelt at her feet in love's wild de·
light.
Oh, for love and for lovers, not since the
sweet air
Has been breathed with their sighs has there
been flower so fair.

IV.

When the Sons of God chose from the
   daughters of men
The sweetest and fairest to be wives to them,
   then
Thy race did begin.   When thy first mother
   was wed,
The stars were made floral to be wreath for
   her head.
Since then I have come, both for bridal and
   bier,
When wand has been lifted, or song sung to
   appear.
Ungava, Ungava, am I needed as breath
In the sweetness of life, or the faintness of
   death ?
Oh, tell me, for ne'er since thy race breathed
   the air
For love and for lovers has there been flower
   so fair."
                              — *From "Ungava."*

DUEL OF THE OLD DUMB CHIEFS.

HEN each his hatchet threw, and all the might of their old withered arms went with the deadly cast. The bright blades whirling on met in mid-flight, and steel and handles shivered at the shock like glass. Then up from either line of faces battle-painted, ochred in panoply of death, rose a shrill yell as the war hatchets shivered, — a sight no warrior standing there had ever seen before, though some were gray in war and scarred with half a hundred battles. But on the heel of that wild yell of thoughtless rage and pride, the prophets of each tribe sent forth a wail, low, wild, and long as is the cry of crouching, shivering hound above the dying hunter, dying in the snow. For well they read the sign, and knew that never yet had warriors lived whose axes met midway between their heads and shivered in the air.

Then the two aged, tongueless foes drew bow and loosened quiver, and quick as lightning's flash set shaft to tightened string. The air between them on the instant thickened with flying shafts; the rounded shields of walrus hide, hung from their necks above each shrivelled breast, rang like two anvils tapped by falling hammers as the steel-headed arrows smote them. So rained and rang the bolts of death upon the two opposing shields, and, when the sheafs were spent, their tawny, shrunken arms and shoulders were cut and pierced with gashes red and deep, and blood fell downward from their wounds as fall the first drops from a cloud before the thunder rolls; while at their feet the feathers

from the broken shafts lay thick
as plumage in a glade above whose
turf two hungry, hunting eagles,
swooping at one prey, have met in
mad and disappointed swoop, and
clinched. But by no bolt had
either shield been pierced, and
underneath the tough, protecting
hides their old mad hearts, un-
touched, beat, hating, on.

Then rose a mighty murmur,
and each line of battle, forgetful
of its hate, swayed in around the
fighters; for never on wild Un-
gava's stormy shore, where bloody
war had been for twice a thousand
years, had there been seen by
mortal eyes such dreadful fight
before. It was as if these two old
chiefs had burst their cerements
of bark and risen out of graves,
shrivelled, dried, death-dumb, to
fight, and show the younger men
that gazed, how their old grand-
sires fought it out. The Trapper,
leaning on his rifle not ten paces
off, saw in the gloomy orbs of the

old Chief the death light shine, and knew that this was his last battle. Thrice lifted he his rifle butt from sand, then drove it back. Thrice did his mighty fingers seek hatchet handle, then fall away, and with a groan he said, —

"Nay. Nay. It may not be. It is a mighty fight and fair. My God! it must go on! But his old eyes will never gaze again on the loved rocks of Mistassinni!"

Thus mingled were both wars. The Esquimau stood side by side with hated Nasquapee. Their painted faces almost touched as they stood thronged around the dreadful two whose hearts were hot with hate, kindled in old fights fought on those barren shores before the warriors round them had been born.

Then once again the old gray haters faced, and their throats rattled, struggling with wild yells. Their sunken eyes glowed hot as burning coals. They dashed their shields to earth and stooped low down. Then drew their knives, long, bright, and keenly edged; sprang into air and met, — and *struck*. Each knife drove, heart-deep, home; and, as they fell apart, each bosom held the other's blade sunk 'twixt the ribs to the strong handle. So they died.—*From " Un-gava."*

NATURAL LAUGHTER.

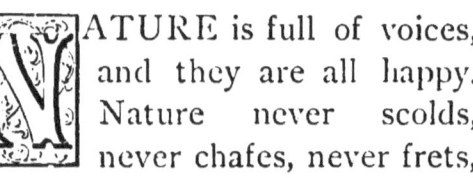ATURE is full of voices, and they are all happy. Nature never scolds, never chafes, never frets, never worries one. She is full of music, and fun and merriment are her delight. I have lain for many an hour hidden amid her leaves and her grasses, and seen denizens of lake and forest act out their natures, unconscious of my observation. I have laughed till tears stood in my eyes to see the playfulness of her fish and her birds, the gambols and mischievous pranks of her animals.

Now, all men are made to laugh. Every man can be tickled if you find the right nerve. No man is so crusty that he won't mellow up

at a picnic, or on a fishing-trip, or
at a fox-hunt. And the laughing
which nature prompts is never
bitter, never cynical. Nature
brings out the real human that lies
latent in one, uncaps the choked-up
springs of merriment in the bosom,
and sets the rivulet of laughter
flowing. The laughter of in-door
life is smothered, constrained,
puckered into forms of politeness;
but the laughter of the out-door life
is large and hearty and thoroughly
jolly. "No one laughs well who
doesn't laugh loud," says the old
proverb; and the proverbs of a
people are the wisdom of a people
condensed. The fact is, the fun-
niest laughter is the laughter that
one has alone. It is very well to
laugh in company, for custom and
benevolence alike demand it; but,
for the most part, company laughter
is forced. It is a made-up, arti-
ficial thing, or else too slight and
decorous to be hearty and adequate.
But when the spirit of fun gets

into one when all alone by himself to such an extent as to fairly possess him, and he sits down and puts his hands against his sides, and opens his mouth, and begins to sway backward and forward until his eyes rain with mirth, and he fairly wrestles inwardly with his hilarity, then his laughter is the genuine thing.—*From "Lake Champlain and its Shores."*

WHY THE OLD TRAPPER NEVER SMOKED.

AKING my pipe from my pocket, I filled it with a choice brand of tobacco I had in my pouch, and proffered it to him.

"Thank ye, thank ye, Henry," said he, as he made a motion of rejection of the offer with his hand, "I thank ye for the kindness ye mean in yer heart, but ef it be all the same to ye, I won't take it. I know it be a comfort to ye, and I am glad to see ye enjoy it, but I have never used the weed; not for the reason that I had a conscience in the matter, but because the Lord gave me a nose like a hound's, and better, too, I dare say, for I doubt ef a hound knows the sweetness of

things, or can take pleasure from
the scent that goes into his nostrils.
But he has been more marciful to
man — as it was proper he should
be — and gin him the power to
know good and evil in the air; and
smellin' has always been one of
my gifts, and I couldn't make ye
understand, I dare say, the pleasure
I've had in the right exercise of it.
For ye know that natur' is no more
bright to the eye than it is sweet
to the nose ; and I've never found
a root or shrub or leaf that hadn't
its own scent.   Even the dry moss
on the rocks, dead and juiceless as
it seems, has a smell to it ; and as
for the 'arth, I love to put my nose
into the fresh sile, as a city woman
loves the nozzle of her smellin'-
bottle.   Many and many a time
when alone here in the woods have
I taken my boat and gone up into
the inlet when the wild roses was
in blossom, or down into some bay
where the white lily cups was all
open, and sot in my boat and smelt

them by the hour, and wondered ef
heaven smelt so. Yis, I have been
sartinly gifted in my nose, for I've
always noted that I smelt things
that the men and women I was
guidin' didn't, and found things in
the air that they never suspicioned
of, and I feered that smokin' might
take away my gift, and that ef I
got the strong smell of tobacco in
my nose once I should never scent
any other smell that was lesser and
finer than it. — So I have never
used the weed, bein' sort of naterally afeered of it ; but what is
medicine for one man may be pisen
for another, as I have noted in
animils, for the bark that fattens
the beaver will kill the rat ; and so
ye must take no offence at what
I've said, but smoke as much as ye
feel moved to, and I will scent the
edges of the smell as it comes over
my side of the fire, and so we'll
sort of jine works — as they say
in the settlements — ye do the
smokin' and I'll do the smellin',

and I think I've got the lightest
end of the stick at that." And
the old man laughed in every line
of his time-wrinkled face at the
smartness of his saying. — *From*
"*Adirondack Tales.*"   *Vol. i.*

ELL, Henry, it was sorter
new work, ye see, for
me and the hound ; for
though I have buried
many a man in the trenches arter
the fight, and though I have kiv-
ered up a good many redskins off
and on in my life, yit I wasn't very
handy at the mournin' equipments
of the settlements. But I have
seed many a gineral laid out on his
bier, in the old wars, with his uni-
form on and his sword by his side,
and the death sentries on duty, and
the muffled drums all beatin', and
I conceited that though Mr. Rob-
erts wasn't a gineral, nor even a
privit in the ranks for that matter,
that he should be treated in an
honorable way now he was dead,

"So I cut some crotches and drove 'em into the ground, and made a frame of small white birches about the size of a bier, and on these I put a layer of balsam and cedar boughs, and over these I scattered pine tufts until I had a bed fit for the dead or livin', gineral or privit, and I laid in plenty of hard wood for my fire, and some pitch knots, for I said to myself, 'Ef the animils come round I will have to shine up on 'em, and defend the corpse;' for I feered the panthers — for this lake be a great spot for the varmints, and 'leven year agone there was sartinly as many as there be now. And arter I had got the bier ready I laid the body on it, and bolstered the head up nateral-like, and then me and the hound sot down to supper, with a dead man at the table. We didn't waste time in the eatin', for the sun was already down, and by the time we had cleaned things up night had come.

"Well, Henry, I took my stand at the foot of the bier, and kept my death-watch, rifle in hand, steady as a sentry on duty, save when I stirred the fire or lighted a pine knot. For the animils was oneasy, as they always be when a corpse is round, and I needed the pine knots more than once, and some of the varmints got the tech of lead and the smell of powder that night, I tell ye, for they was full of their divilments, and made me and the hound as wakeful as ef we was surrounded by inimies."

"Did you really have to kill anything?" I asked, speaking for the first time in an hour; for the Old Trapper had told his story with such naturalness of intonation and gesture that he had held me spellbound by his narrative — for no one could hear him tell the strange tale he was telling, and not be carried along by the movement of it, — and now that he was evidently reaching the climax, I feared I

should miss some detail of his
experience which, being omitted,
would mar the narration, so, hop-
ing to hold his utterance to the
line of actual occurrence, I said,
"Did you have to kill anything
that night?"

"Well, yis, I did," he replied.
"I bored a hole through a dog wolf
over there on the beach, arter I had
borne his onnateral howlin' as long
as a mortal could, and I dropped a
cat from that dead cedar, arter me
and the hound had stood the stare
of her eyes for ten minutes or more,
and about two in the mornin', a
litter of panthers crawled in on us
ontil the bush seemed alive with
'em, and I lifted the scalp of the
biggest of the drove, arter he had
got within forty feet of the corpse
and paid no more attention to the
brands I pitched at him than ef
they was tufts of sod; so, with a
pine knot all afire in one hand, to
show me the sights, I drove the
lead in between his infarnal eyes

in a style that taught 'em all manners for the rest of the watch.
Yis, Henry, we had a solemn and
lively time of it, for sartin, that
night, and at times it looked as ef
there would be no funeral the next
day, leastways, none that me and
the hound would attend, onless we
made one for ourselves, but we
stood to our post, and between the
brands and the lead and the help
of the Lord we brought the body
through safe 'til sunrise.

"But it was mighty solemn
watchin' by the body all by myself
on the shores of this lake here
that night; for at times the animils would make the air roar and
scream, and the mountains to yelp
as ef the upper world was inhabited
with cats and wolves and panthers,
and then they would suddenly become quiet, and the world round
about was nothin' but silence with
the moon shinin' through it; and
the dead man's face was white
as the moon and still as the air,

for his troubles was over and the marks of them passed from his featur's when his breath went away. And so me and the hound kept our watch by the dead, 'til the sun riz in the east, and the hour had come for the funeral." — *From "Adirondack Tales." Vol. i.*

HE evening passed like a sweet song through dewy air. She was so full of health, so richly gifted, so happy in her heart, so nigh to wedded life with him she worshipped, that her soul was full of joyousness, as the lark's throat, soaring skyward, is of song. She chattered like a magpie in many tongues, translating rare old bits of foreign wit and ancient mirth with apt and laughable grimaces. Her face was mobile, rounding with jollity or lengthening with woe at will. She had the light foot and the pliant limb, the superb pose, abandon, and the languishing repose of her old race, whose princesses, with velvet feet, tinkling ankles, and forms voluptuous, lithe

as snakes, danced before kings and
won kingdoms with applause from
those whom, by their wheeling,
swaying, flashing beauty, they
made wild. She danced the dances
of the East, when dancing was a
language and a worship, with pan-
tomime so rare and eloquent that
the pleased eye translated every
motion, as the ear catches the
quick speech. Then sang she the
old songs of buried days, sad, wild,
and sweet as love singing at death's
door to memory and to hope ; the
song of joys departed and of joys
to come. So passed the evening
till the eastern stars, wheeling upward, stood in the zenith. Then
with lingering lips she kissed her
lover on the mouth, and on her
couch of fragrant boughs fell fast
asleep, forgetful of all things but
life and love ; murmuring softly in
her happy dreams, " To-morrow
night," and after a little space,
again, " Sweet, sweet to-morrow ! "
— *From " Mamelons.*

ENRY," said the old man, as he drew his hunting-knife through the tender-loin roll, and marked the ruddy juices that oozed out, and the puff of odorous steam which ascended as the blade clove it, "this meat is cooked hunter-like, and sort of encourages the teeth to git into the centre of it. I have often noted that cookin' was a kind of gift, and couldn't be larnt out of books, no more than holdin' a rifle or featherin' a paddle properly can be larnt in the settlements. The Lord gives one man one set of gifts and another another, and cookin' and huntin' be things of natur', and not of readin', and they don't often go all of them to one

man, although in yer case, Henry, the Lord has been very marciful and gracious-like in his treatment of ye, — for I have heerd, ye be a great scholar, and love the knowledge that the schools give ; and I have many things I want to ax ye of — things I have heerd, but that seem onreasonable to me ; but, depend on it, Henry, the best gift the Lord has gin ye is yer love of natur' and the things that go with it — a keen eye, a quick finger, a strong back, and a conscience that can meet him in the solitude of these waters and hills and not be afeerd ; for a wicked man can't bear the presence of the Maker of these solitudes, as I have good reason to know" — and here the old man paused a moment and gazed steadily into the fire. " Yis," he resumed, " it be wonderful that he should have gin ye the love of books and of natur' both, but I dare to say he has his favorites, as I have often noticed mothers have among their childun, and I can see jest how it may be with him ; but how he came to gin ye the gift of cookin' with all the other ones, is wonderful, and I can't understand it." — *From " Adirondack Tales."* *Vol. i.*

CHAMPLAIN'S ENTRANCE INTO THE
LAKE.

IT was the 3d of July, 1609, when Champlain first gazed upon the lake which subsequently bore his name, and which to-day is the sole monument that perpetuates his fame. We do not know certainly the exact hour, but it was early in the morning when the canoe which bore him glided out from between the overhanging maples and cedars which lined either bank of the Richelieu, and entered the broader waters of the lake. The spectacle which met his eyes was one which brought exclamations of astonishment from his mouth, and as his canoe swept onward over the level water new

beauties and wider expanses of
natural loveliness broke upon his
view. Even then he was a world-
wide traveller. He had visited
Mexico, Vera Cruz, and Panama.
The luxuriant loveliness of the
tropics and the more sober beauties of semi-tropical regions were
familiar to him. He had seen the
best that the continent of Europe
had to show. He had gazed upon
the green meadows of Acadia and
the awful grandeurs of the Saguenay. But never before had he
looked upon a scene of such picturesque beauty, and such varied
loveliness, as this body of water
presented to his appreciative eyes
as it lay revealed in the dewy light
of this warm July morning.

Not a breath was moving in the
air. The lake, between its widen-
ing shores, stretched before him
smooth as glass. Through it the
noiseless paddles moved the noiseless bark in which he stood and
gazed. Behind him came the

twenty-four canoes, silently follow-
ing his silent wake. The paddles
rose and sank in perfect unison.
The ochred faces of the Indians
and their feathered scalp-locks
showed brilliantly in the morning
light. The air was odorous with
the perfumes of gums and flowers.
Here and there lilies starred the
water whitely. Large fish leaped,
splashed, and drove their sharpened wedge of motion along the
level surface. Through the dewy
air came the pure, sweet note of the
hermit thrush. Far overhead the
hunting eagle, sweeping round and
round in watchful circles, came to
a sudden stop, fluttered for a
moment, and then, with rightly
balanced poise, drove headlong
downward into the lake. Ducks
blackened the water for acres. The
mother does watched the playful
fawns bounding along the sand.
The lumbering moose waded la-
boriously shoreward, and on the
marshy bank stood at gaze. Above,

the sky was sapphire. Over the
eastern mountains the sun showed
redly. The mighty woods came to
the water's edge, an unbroken
mass of natural forest. The lake,
to which he was to give his name
while living, that was to be his
everlasting monument when dead,
welcomed his entrance between
her shores with the finest expres-
sions of her loveliness. Champlain had come to his own, and his
own received him gladly. — *From
"Lake Champlain and its Shores."*

THE YANKEE AS A TRAVELLER.

E four — the Inseparables, as the Man from New Hampshire facetiously called us — left Banff with bright anticipations. Our eyes were as open to see and our spirits as buoyant as if we were boys. We had had a week of pleasure at the "Palace of De-light," as the Judge poetically named the huge hostelry among the mountains, and our last night had been one of rollicking enjoy-ment. In our dispositions we typed the best habit of Americans when travelling — the habit of self-surrender to the enjoyment of the hour. There can be no question on one point concerning our countrymen. They are the

best travellers in the world, not
because they travel the most and
spend money the freest when
journeying, but because they get
more knowledge and happiness out
of travel than any other people.
The inconveniences and depriva-
tions which roughen the temper of
the average Englishman only
quicken the humor of the Yankee
and supply him with entertainment. He travels as a bird flies,
utilizing to his enjoyment the
opposition of adverse currents,
feeds contentedly on the wing,
and sleeps restfully on any perch
to which the flaws or whirlwinds
of unlucky happenings by day or
night have gustily blown him.
The world likes him and he likes
the world, and hence he finds welcome everywhere, and the welcome
he gets he thoroughly enjoys.
Like a snail, he carries his home
around with him on his back, and
easily adjusts himself to any condition of shine or shade. The

happiest mortal one can meet with
is an American in his travels.
Speaking but one language and
that indifferently well, he hobnobs
cheerfully with all nations, uses
with the courage of ignorance all
languages, and makes fast friends
wherever he goes. — *From " Daylight Land."*

HERE is no other word in the vocabulary of our language so suggestive of rare and pleasant conditions of living as camping. It is more than a mere word ; it is a symbol as well. It stands for a class of experiences so fresh, novel, and healthy that it is beloved by imagination and memory alike. It is so truly a mirror to many of us that in it, as in a glass, we see trees, the shores of lovely lakes, the banks of quietly flowing rivers, wooded islands around which the waves run caressingly, beaches of gleaming sand, and ranges of lofty mountains. In it, also, are cabins of bark, camp-fires that crackle, and blaze, and flare red lights high

up amid swaying branches, and
widely out in a great circle through
the dark forest. And in the word
are faces and forms that have been
companions with us in our forest
wanderings, some of whom are
with us to this day, and other ones
that are not now with us, nor will
they ever be again on this earth,
and, alas! we know not where they
are.

Not only is it a word for the
eye, but it is equally a word for the
ear. For in it are the sighing of
zephyrs, the soft intoning of slow-
moving night winds, the roaring
of strong gales, the moaning of
tempests, and the sobbings of
storms among the wet trees. The
loon's call, the splash of leaping
fish, the panther's cry, the pitiful
summons of the lost hound, the
slashing of deer wading among the
lily pads, and the soft dripping of
odorous gums falling gently on the
pine stems, listening to which in
silence and sweet content, we, who

were lying under the fragrant trees, like happy and weary children, have fallen gently asleep, — all these sounds live in the word as music lives forever in the air of heaven, being a part of it.

And in it too are human voices, songs, laughter, and all the happy noises of merriment and frolic. No other phonograph is like to it. The happy hunter's proud hurrah over the captured game ; the songs around the camp-fire under the stars in the hush of evening ; the stranger's hail ; the guide's strong call to breakfast, a heavenly sound — the flute's soft note across the water on a still night ; the cheer on reaching camp, and the mur-mured farewells at leaving ; verily, it is a vocal word, and all the sounds that come from it are melody.

Dear word, sweet word, keep vocal to my ears until they cease to hear, and mirror to my eyes until they see no more the fair, the sweet, and the honest faces that

out of the dear old camps that we
have builded in so many parts for
so many years, now look forth
upon me as out of many heavens.
For if there be a better heaven
than a well-placed camp with a
wisely assorted company of honest
and cheerful folk, I know not how
to find it in my imagination nor
that passage of Revelation that
tells us of it.

TREES AT VANCOUVER.

UT of such a forest a site for Vancouver City has been hewn. It cost three hundred dollars per acre to merely fell and burn the gigantic growth. When we arrived, only two trees were still standing, and they were burning like a blast furnace, inside their hollow trunks. They were nearly three hundred feet in height and measured between thirty and forty feet in circumference. For one hundred and fifty feet they rose like mammoth pillars of wood, straight as a plumb line, bare of branch or knot. Our artist sketched them on the spot only an hour before they fell with a sweep, a rush, and a roar of sound as if the columns which

uphold the sky had slipped from
their bases and a section of heaven
had dropped suddenly — a vast
ruin — to the earth. The earth
trembled to the shock of their
overthrow, the air groaned, and as
the roar of their fall rolled across
the level water of Burrard's Inlet,
through the still air, the mountains
beyond sent back the murmurs of
their regret. Alas, that life must
forever feed its growth on death,
and human progress advance only
over the ruins of the perfect!

They fell, and the saws went at
them. How their senseless, hungry, cruel teeth ate into and destroyed the majesty of their sublime proportions! We turned
away, from a sense of pain and
sheer vexation. In the evening
the Judge and I crept up through
the *débris* and heavy semi-tropical
undergrowth to the crown of the
hill on which they had stood. The
warm evening air was filled with a
ruddy glow, for a hundred giant

stumps were still feebly gasping
forth fire.   We lighted two resin-
ous torches and counted the rings
which would give us the measure
of their age.

"*Six hundred and seventy-four
years old!*" gasped the Judge, and
he dropped his torch to the ground.
"My God! these trees were older
than the landing of Columbus,
older than Magna Charta, older
than the first translation of the
Bible into English, and last week
they stood with a thousand years
of life ahead of them, and these
men of Vancouver have levelled
them to the earth with as little
sense of what they were doing as
the Vandals had when they over-
turned the immortal sculptures of
Rome, and trampled the triumphs
of art under the hoofs of their
chargers!   It is simply brutal.
But the trees will have long and
sure revenge."

"How is that?" I queried, as I
flung my torch away in rage at

what had been done, for I shared
the indignation of my companion.
" How will these thoughtless people be punished for this wanton
deed ? "

" Mr. Murray," cried the Judge
in reply, " Boston would give a
million of dollars to have two such
trees, growthful and strong with
six centuries of growth and ten
centuries of life ahead of them on
her Common.   What would London give for two such monuments?
What Paris?   Had these Vancouver men had the reverence or wit
to have set apart a space six hundred feet across for a small park
on this knoll, — the very centre
and crown of their city, that is to
be, — they would have made it the
Mecca of thousands upon thousands of visitors each year.   That
railroad there could have afforded
to pay a million of dollars to have
kept these two gigantic trees, these
majestic monuments of past centuries, built up from the soil, the

air, and the sunshine, by the Lord,
standing here. There is not a
sculpture, shaft, or fresco in Rome,
that can compare with these trees
as they stood but yesterday in
their attractiveness to the eyes
and the imagination of men.
These trees thus preserved would
have made their city one of the
noted cities of the world. Every
pen that came hither would have
written of them ; every pencil
have sketched them ; every brush
made them the foreground of this
magnificent view ; every tongue
told of them to listening ears far
away. The Bank of England put
at their disposal could not buy for
them such an advertisement as
these two trees gave them free of
cost. And now they lie in these
hot ashes lost to the world forever,
burning as if they were an offence
to the eye, a stench to the senses,
a collection of offal. What a pity,
what a loss ! Come, let us get
away from this spot. The air is

filled with the reproach of the
centuries that look upon their
highest artistic result as despised
and rejected of men. I shall
always think of Vancouver as I
should of Rome if St. Peter's
were destroyed by a mob." —
From "Daylight Land."

THE TRAPPER'S PARTING WITH HIS DOGS.

THAT same hour, four miles down the Raquette, a passer would have seen a boat drawn up into a little creek that emptied itself into the river at the base of an over-hanging hill. Had he landed, prompted by curiosity, and fol-lowed a trail that led through the marsh grass, some forty rods be-yond, he would have come upon a man seated on the banks of the stream at the foot of a pine, with two dogs, lying one on his right hand, the other on his left, with their muzzles resting on either leg. Could the man have crept near enough to hear the words that were being spoken, he would have heard the Trapper say, —

"It be a leetle hard, pups, yis, it sartinly be a leetle hard, for a man at my time of life to be parted from his dogs, considerin' the time we've consorted together, and the comfort we be to each other. But the vagabonds have sworn to pizen ye, and though ye be sensible pups, yit natur' is natur', and it's onreasonable to think that ye would refuse to eat. Leastwise, Rover, I conceit that ye would sartinly make a fool of yerself and eat meat from a man's hand ef ye knowed it was pizen. I've better thought of Sport, for the lad was a timid boy, and didn't consort with strangers, and a dog's ways be the ways of his master, as I've noted, and I sartinly think that Sport would be more reasonable and even show his teeth to the vagabonds ef they tempted him.

"And now, pups" said the old man, as he rose to his feet, "there is no tellin' when we three meet agin, for the vagabonds will be up to their diviltry, and the boy isn't here. Here is meat enough to last ye a week, ef ye be reasonable in yer appetite, but ef ye be wasteful ye'll sartinly fast without credit to ye afore the week be ended. The water is within reach, and ef wust comes to wust, and the man that leaves ye don't come back to ye, ye can use yer teeth on the thong, and take yer own course to the camp. The boy will find yer there when he comes in, and yer noses will keep ye alive till then. I shall sartinly try to sarcumvent the vagabonds, but my years be many and it may be the Lord's time to call has come. But I sha'n't go till I'm sartin he's in 'arnest and I've helped him out a leetle in his management of the vagabonds on the Pint. And now, pups," said the old man again, as he turned to go, "I say good-by to ye, not knowin' what'll happen. Ef ye come back to the cabin and

find me one way, it'll be all right.
Ef ye come back to the cabin and
find me another way, why, then, do
ye stay by the cabin till the boy
comes in, and then it will be all
right ; for he'll know what to do
with me, and he'll know what to
do for ye, for we talked both mat-
ters over afore our last partin'.
Yis, yis," said the Trapper to himself, as he turned back on his trail
and started to his boat, "it'll be all
right whichever way the pups find
me ; but it's hard for a man of my
years to be parted from his dogs."

SABBATH IN THE WOODS.

F a person would know how sensitive his nature is, how readily it responds to every exhibition of beauty and power, how thoroughly adapted it is, in all its faculties, to religious impressions, he must leave the haunts of men, — where every sight and sound distracts his attention, and checks the free exercises of his soul, — and, amid the silence of the woods, hold communion with his Maker. It is the *silence* of the wilderness which most impresses me. The hours of the Sabbath pass noiselessly. No voice of conversation, no sound of hurrying feet, no clangor of bells, no roll of wheels, disturbs your meditations. You do not feel like

reading or talking or singing. The heart needs neither hymn nor prayer to express its emotions. Even the Bible lies at your side unlifted. The letters seem dead, cold, insufficient. You feel as if the very air was God, and you had passed into that land where written revelation is not needed ; for you see the Infinite as eye to eye, and feel him in you and above you and on all sides. It is true, at intervals, you turn to the Bible. You have your reading moods, when some apt passage, some ap-propriate selection or chapter, is read, with a profit and rapture never before experienced. But this mood I believe to be the exception. Ordinarily, the spirit is above the letter. The action of eye and voice interferes with the sentiment. You do not want to read, but think. When you feel the presence of a friend, have his hand in yours, see him at your very side, you do not need to take up a

letter and read that he is with you.
So with God : in the silence of the
woods the soul apprehends him
instinctively. He is everywhere.
In the fir and pine, which, like the
tree of life, shed their leaves every
month, and are forever green ; in
the water at your feet, which no
paddle has ever vexed and no taint
polluted, rivalling that which is as
"pure as crystal ;" in the mountains, which, in every literature,
have been associated with the
Deity, you see Him who of old time
was conceived of as a "Dweller
among the hills." With such
symbols and manifestations of God
around, you need not go to 'the
lettered page to learn of him. The
Bible, with its print and paper, is
a hindrance rather than a help.
Like a glass with too narrow a
field, it concentrates the vision too
much. It clips the wings of the
imagination, and narrows the circle
of its flight. The spirit which, for
the first time perhaps, has escaped

the bonds of formal worship, for the first time tasted of freedom and tested its capacities to soar, returns regretfully to the restraint and bondage of book and speech. It takes these up as an angel, whose hands have once swept a heavenly harp, touches again the strings of an earthly instrument.— *From "Adventures in the Wilderness."*

THE TRAPPER'S MATCH WITH THE
GAMBLER.

YE can say what ye've got
to say," answered the
Trapper. "Ye can say
what ye've got to say,
young man, but I don't conceit
that the signs pint towards peace,
for there be a right and a wrong
about it, and that makes bargainin'
out of the question, as I jedge."

"I tell you what I will do,"
responded the gambler; "I'll draw
with you for it;" and as he spoke
he shuffled all the face cards out of
the pack on to the ground. "You
don't understand the value of the
pictures, but you do know that two
is more than one and ten more
than five. If you draw higher than
I, you shall not be disturbed; if I

draw higher than you, you sha'n't disturb us. Come, how do you like that ? "

" I. don't do things that way," answered the Trapper. " When I *draw*, as ye call it, it will be in a different fashion."

For a moment the gambler stood perplexed, and an expression almost of pain crossed his handsome features, and the customary nonchalance of his manner sobered into gravity, and then he said, —

" Old man, the game has got to stop ; it's all one-sided and it is simply murder. I will give you a second plan, and for God's sake don't say nay to it ! There is a man about your age down on the coast, — he and I have not had much to do with each other for some years. You see, we had a little conversation one evening, and I left that night. I have not seen him since. He's about your age ; your head makes me think of him. There is a slight relationship be-

tween us; they call it Father, I
think. Well, no matter about that;
I want to stop this thing right here,
and this is what I propose: You
see those pistols — they are favorites of mine. I say plainly, that
there is but one man in the world
to whom I cannot give odds and
win. I know your skill, and the
piece that lies in your arm is, I
suppose, your favorite. I tell you
what we will do. If you won't
draw for it, we will shoot for it.
Any way so that the cards sha'n't
be stocked, old man, — any way so
that the cards won't be stocked;"
and then the man, after a moment's
pause, said, "Will you shoot for
it?"

"What's the match?" asked the
Trapper.

"Do you mean what is the
prize?" interrogated the gambler.

"Sartin, sartin," answered the
Trapper, "a man don't want to
barn powder for nothin', not to
speak of the caps and the lead,

though the caps be plenty and the boy sends the lead in by the ton."

"The prize is this," answered the gambler: "we will shoot three shots; if I win, you are to let the camp alone; if you win, the game goes on, — if you choose. What say you to that?"

"The matter of shootin'," answered the Trapper, "is a kind of pleasant divarsion to a man of my gifts at this time of the year, when the bucks be lean, the does with fawn, and the fur loose in the skin. And ef ye want a leetle playfulness, why, the air be clear and the light jest about right; and as for yer pistil shootin', Henry has told me a good deal off and on about the tricks that the perfessers have, and it may be ye can show an old man some new devices and a surer way to drive lead than he has larnt in sixty year of practice with the weepon. Yis, ye name yer targets, and we'll shoot the three shots, and ef ye beat me at the shootin',

I'll take the pups and start for the Saranac afore ye can paddle yer canoe to yer camp ; for the boy be comin' in soon, and the Lord knows I wouldn't have him see the man that beat me shootin' when I was usin' the powder and the lead and the caps he has sent me.   Yis, I'll accept the tarms."

The angel that keeps the book in which the emotions of the human heart are recorded will surely remember in the hour of his deepest need the flush of satisfaction that lighted the pale face of the gambler and the joy that leapt to his heart as the old man, whose whitened head had reminded him of his distant and deserted father, closed with his proposition. He turned toward his canoe with a foot swift and light as a boy's when buoyant with happiness, for, knowing his own almost matchless skill, he felt confident of winning the match and thus saving from murderous violence the old man to

whom his heart had, as he con-
versed with him, more and more
strongly gone out. With a fine
touch of chivalry, which the Trapper was not slow to notice, the
gambler left one pistol in the boat,
and, returning, with equal chivalry
proposed to shoot the first shot
himself.

"Ye needn't think that I mis-
trust ye, boy, for I don't," said the
Trapper. "But it may be the
thought of my faith in ye will
make yer narves steadier in the
trial, — make it seem more like a
leetle playfulness atween us, and
not a matter of life and death, as
it's pretty sartin to be, so pick yer
target and show us the natur' of
yer gifts. Lord-a-massy, ef the
boy was here, what fun we three
would have!"

"This is the first trial," said the
man. "You see two cones on that
pine, — the two that stand tipping
the third branch from the water.
I will take the lower. If it is left,

you can take it," said the gambler laughingly; "if not, the other," and as the last word sounded, his pistol cracked sharp and quick and the little cone, no larger than a marble, disappeared.

"Ye did it well," said the Trapper. "I've picked that tree nearly clean myself; but I will take the one ye left;" and the vibrations of the last word were lost in the ring of the piece as he discharged it.

The gambler looked at the twig now bare, then he looked at the Trapper, and said, —

"Honors are easy, old man," and he laughed like a boy; but through the laughter quivered a vibration of graver quality, almost of pain.

In a moment each of the two men had reloaded his weapon, and the Trapper said, —

"What next, friend?"

"This," answered the gambler, and walking off some twenty paces, he put a deuce of spades against a

stump, and returning, he said, " I
take the lower," and again his pistol
cracked, quick as thought.

"And I take the upper," said
the Trapper, and his bullet drove
through the upper spot, as the
gambler's had through the lower.

Again they recharged their
pieces.

" What next ? " asked the Trapper. " There is only one more
bullet, and it isn't sartin whether I
go to the Saranac or to the ·Pint."

" Say, rather, old man, that it is
not certain whether you go to the
Saranac or to your death," almost
solemnly reiterated the gambler.

" The Lord beyend doubt
knows," answered the Trapper ;
" but the shootin' may help him
decide."

But the humor of the Trapper
started no answering smile on the
face of the gambler. He said not
a word, but took two glass balls
brightly gilded from his pocket,
and, giving one to the Trapper, he
said, —

"A flying shot. I never missed but once!" And steadying himself for a moment, he breathed his breath from his chest and tossed the shining globe high into the air. Up, up it went ; another second and it would reach the apex of its upward flight, at which point the Trapper knew full well the gambler had calculated to take it. Was it fate, was it Providence, was it the gambler's "luck," that even at the instant when it came to the point of its highest flight, a puff of wind caught it suddenly and blew it outward as if it were a feather, and the bullet from the gambler's pistol missed it by its width ?

But another bullet did not miss it, for scarcely had the pistol cracked before the Trapper jumped his rifle to his cheek, and as the wind swept the shining globe out over the lake, his bullet caught it as it flew, and the globe burst into gilded fragments.

" *The game goes on,*" said the

gambler, and he turned carelessly toward the canoe; but his face was white in its excitement, though not a muscle moved. He had nearly reached the canoe when he turned, and, stepping quickly back in front of the Trapper, he said, —

"Look here, old man, the game will go against you; for the cards are stocked and you stand no chance. I thought to stop the play and save your life; but for the first time in years luck has turned against me, and when we meet again we meet as enemies. Still, I like the way you hold your cards; and though you play a lone hand — one against seven — still luck may pull you through, so, not knowing how 'twill end, we'll part man style. Your heart is right, your eye sure, and your finger quick, and though I'm in for it and shall play the game through and kill you if I can, yet, in my heart, old whitehead, I trust to God you'll win."

E wear out too fast, friends, in this country. We value ourselves too much as if we were bits of machinery. Our lives ascend like the rocket — suddenly explode and leave darkness. They should rise like the sun in gradual ascension, and decline with the even movement of unexhausted powers passing on into other realms. The problem of the next thirty years, in this country, is not one of money-making, or of mind-making, or of soul-making, but the problem is one that underlies all these, and on the proper solution of which they all depend — it is body-making. The births of the future must be healthy births. What is the

use of bringing cripples into the
world, whether they are crippled in
limb, in stomach, in size and formation of the chest, or in the
blood-system? As a country, we
are giving birth to a monstrous
number of idiots and weaklings,
and of incipient, embryo criminals.
We can't afford to keep on taxing
our industries with their support,
imperilling society with their violence, or burdening our sympathies
with their presence. Healthy
parentage is a solution of this
problem. You can't expect that
nervous motherhood and fevered
fatherhood will ever stand parents
to healthy offspring. The laws of
life, about which the average man
and woman are so ignorant, should
be taught and obeyed as the ten
commandments, for the next fifty
years. From the great out-doors
of God, — pure air, strong wind,
warm sunshine, plain diet, restful
periods of time, and the religious
sensitiveness which is closely con-

nected with these influences of
Nature, — from these must come
our salvation. If we would brick
up the flues of our furnaces and
put the old-fashioned fireplace, or
even the open grate, into the rooms
of our houses, we would prove by
that act that our civilization, at
least, isn't stupid, and that we are
too sensible to pay men for killing
us with their infernal inventions.
— *From " Lake Champlain and its
Shores."*

THE AMBUSH.

ORNING came. There was a man crouched back of a bowlder in the rear of the outlaws' camp who, with eyes that had never closed, and with ears strained with intense effort of hearing, had, through the hours of the night, waited patiently for the coming of the day. That man was John Norton the Trapper.

It was his eye that first saw the new shade of color come to the fog that hung heavily over the lake ; his eye noted the first movement amid the mist, and greeted the light with bright and eager anticipation. He was not a man to desert a comrade, and it was evident, by the look on his face that if any harm had come

to the Yankee, some of the vagabonds, as he mentally expressed it,
would have to answer for it.

All humor — and his face was
capable of expressing supreme
humor — all amiable expression,
and the sweet peacefulness that
had become habitual in the later
years to his countenance, had departed, and in their place the face
showed, in the morning light, a set
and rigid look. The lines were
taut around the mouth, and the
eyes that looked out from under
the heavy eyebrows gleamed hard
and cold as steel. One man
against seven. One man under
cover in a position that commanded the whole camp, unless
the occupants lay close, with a
rifle in his hand, waiting for the
coming light ; waiting for a man
to show his head.

Well did those in the camp know
what the light would bring, for the
half-breed in the council held in
the night had told the gambler

that when the sun arose John Norton would have the whole camp within range of his piece, and that to show a head or even a hand would be dangerous. Each man held his place, therefore, armed and ready for fight. The gambler with a pistol in his hand — the one he had used in his match with the Trapper on the beach — stood at the edge of the beach back of a huge pine, the others, each behind his own protection, lay, crouched or stood, according to the necessities of his position.

The Yankee was near the centre of the camp in plain view to all, his body lashed at the shoulders to a dead tamarack, and his hands tied to the tree likewise. It must be confessed that he presented a laughable spectacle, thus trussed up as it were. His back was toward the lake. Perhaps his enemies had placed him so, that he might not see what was going on in the camp. Be that as it

may, his face faced the woods and
commanded an easy view of John
Norton himself, as he crouched
back of his protecting bowlder.
Such was the position of the
several parties when the sun
broke triumphantly through the
fog, which, up to that moment, had
made objects twenty feet distant
invisible.

A glance told the Trapper the
condition of the camp, and the
position of every one of his
enemies. His mind, quick to
decide and full of expedients
gathered by years of experience
in similar emergencies, reached
its conclusions in a moment, and
prompted him to do one of those
unexpected and reckless things,
which, done by any other man,
would be his death, but which,
done by one like him, must, by the
coolest judgment, be pronounced
the only way to success. But first
he would learn the condition of his
captured companion.

"Boy," he said, speaking in a full, steady tone, easily heard through the camp; "boy," he said, "have the vagabonds tetched a hair of yer head?"

"Not a hair," answered Jim Bean. "Every hair, old man, is in the right place, stiff as ever, darn ef it ain't!"

The Yankee had evidently, amid his tribulations, retained both the reckless carelessness of his spirit and the rough humor of his expression.

"It is well," answered the Trapper. "It is well that the dogs have left ye untetched; fer ef they had hurt a hair of yer head, their blood would have answered for it. It is years sence I've felt as I do this mornin'; and ef the vagabonds want lead, lead. they can have. Now, boy, do as I tell ye, and a man who cares nothing fer his life this mornin' will show ye a trick that ye'll remember when ye be gone from the woods. The vagabonds be fools to tie a man of yer inches to a tree whose roots the fire has barnt under."

The old man paused a moment; he drew his knife, holding its handle in his left hand so that it was little impeded in the use which a rapid shot would demand of it; meditated a moment, glanced at the caps and tubes of his rifle, and then he said, calling loud and clear, —

"Who be the spokesman of this camp?, Ef there be a man ye sneaks can trust to speak for ye, let him make himself known."

And then, after a moment's pause, he repeated, "Who be the spokesman of this camp?"

For an instant there was no reply, and then the gambler, from his position behind the pine some fifty yards distant, directly in front of the Trapper, said, —

"I make this deal, old man; if you want to cut, say so!"

"Ay, ay," answered the Trapper, clearly and sharply. "I know yer voice, and well it is that two feet of good pine is atween ye and the line of my lead, for ye have consorted with the wicked in their wickedness, and the punishment of the wicked must rest on yer head. It's well that ye speak fer the vagabonds, fer ye had a leetle playfulness with me the other day, and ye know that my bullets go quick and go straight. And here I say that I know the position of every one of ye, and my eye takes ye all in ; and ef one of ye shows yer head, or enough of yer skull to match the width of a bullet, it will be matched with a bullet, fer I have something to do, so keep yer heads and yer hands out of sight, or ye will lose head or hand. There be seven agin one, but the two of the seven that lift from yer covers fust be dead men. That will leave but five and the chances."

"What do you propose to do?"

asked the gambler coolly, from behind the pine.

"This," answered the Trapper.
And as the word escaped his lips,
he leaped the bowlder behind
which he was crouched, and
landed lightly as a cat on his
feet in full view, knife in hand,
and rifle at a poise ready to shoot.

"Now," he yelled, "show a
head, show a hand ef ye dare!"

The action was so quick, so unexpected, so startlingly bold, the
outlaws and the gambler himself,
were appalled. Their dreaded
enemy was on the margin of their
'camp, and the dreaded rifle had
every position under its muzzles.

Not an instant did the Trapper
lose. No sooner had he given the
warning than he said to the Yankee, who was standing lashed to
the tree, with his mouth fairly
open in astonishment at the Trapper's sudden appearance, —

"Boy, bend yerself forard, and
sot yer strength on to the roots as
ef ye was liftin' a ton."

The Yankee's mouth, as we have said, was open ; it closed. The expression which came to his face was that of quickest intelligence. The look of a man who understands the reason of what he has been told to do, and is mortified that he had not thought of it before. His feelings were of the strongest kind beyond doubt, for the expression with which he eased himself of them was the most earnest in his vocabulary. He said, —

" I sweow ! "

And then, bowing himself forward, while the roots cracked at his feet, he put the full force of his body to the effort he was called upon to make. He lifted it slowly, for the roots hung, but liberty was ahead and an uncertain fate behind him. Every ounce of power that was anywhere lying around in the ungainly length of his entire proportions he put into the effort. The cords cut into his wrists until the blood started, but grit to the last, he never flinched. The last root finally yielded to the strain that he put upon it, and Jim Bean, with the tree whose top reached twenty feet above his head, stood, ready for the next move.

The old Trapper took a step, — one motion of his knife, and the cords were severed. The tree fell with a crash, and Jim Bean was free.

"Scoot, boy," said the Trapper; "use yer legs; head fer the boat beyend the big pine, and ef any- thing happens, make fer the Saranac."

"Not this year, old man; ef there is any wrastlin' goin' on here this mornin', Jim Bean is jest goin' to sidle into it! There is a chap that kicked me in the ribs last night jest for whistlin' a little tune, and I want to get my paw on him for a minit."

"Boy," said the Trapper, "ye

be foolish. Make use of yer legs
and show the Lord by yer runnin'
that ye be grateful for yer deliver-
ance ! "

" I go when you go, old man,"
said the Yankee ; " we came into
this camp together, and we go out
together. We boss this town
meetin' between us, and when you
say adjourn, we'll adjourn, and not
be " —

The word was drowned in the
explosion of the Trapper's rifle.
While the Yankee had been talking, the muzzle of a duelling pistol
had been pushed slowly from behind the pine. The quick eye of
the Trapper had caught the movement ; and before the muzzles had
gotten the line his piece cracked
its report out, and a pistol, struck
square in the muzzle by the bullet,
was knocked from the hand that
held it, twenty feet into the air,
and fell muzzle foremost into the
sand.

" Ye have got yer lesson," said

the Trapper, "ye have got yer
lesson, and it will help ye to credit
the words I tell ye. There's one
bullet left, and ef there be one of
ye that wants to die in the next
twenty seconds, let him lift his
head from his cover."

So saying, the old man backed
his way out of the camp until he
came to the cover of the trees,
behind one of which he glided, the
Yankee taking another.

"Here I be, ye vagabonds!"
shouted the Trapper, as he drove
a bullet into the empty barrel with
a single motion of the rod. "Here
,I be," he repeated, "one man agin
seven, and the trees of the Lord
for a kiver. Come out and show
yerselves and prove yerselves to be
better than sneaks. I come to this
Pint for a parpose, and I don't go
from this Pint till I find out yer
divilments, onless the Lord" —

The sentence was never ended.
To the north a rifle cracked. The
report cut through the atmosphere

like a bullet. The old man flung a hand upward, while his face showed the look of a hound who has suddenly heard the motions of his game.

Quick, alert, eager. Had he been chiselled in marble, his posture could not have been steadier or his pose more rigidly held. An instant, and then a rifle cracked again, — a twin report to the one that had preceded it.

The old man dashed the hand that was still suspended in the air, to his side, and with a voice whose sound was between a sob and a laugh, exclaimed, —

"*Henry!* To the boat! To the boat! The boy and the rifle be both in the woods!"

And then, as if the swiftness of his youth had returned to his frame, the old man, with his rifle at a trail, and his white hair streaming behind him, followed by his companion, who strove vainly to match his velocity, tore wildly toward the boat. — *From "Adirondack Tales." Vol. ii.*

HUS were they seated, ready to begin the repast ; but the plates remained untouched, and the happy noises which had to that moment filled the cabin ceased ; for the Angel of Silence, with noiseless step, had suddenly entered the room. There's a silence ، of grief, there's a silence of hatred, there's a silence of dread ; of these, men may speak, and these they can describe. But the silence of our happiness, who can describe that ? When the heart is full, when the long longing is suddenly met, when love gives to love abundantly, when the soul lacketh nothing and is content, — then language is useless, and the Angel

of Silence becomes our only
adequate interpreter. A humble
table, surely, and humble folk
around it ; but not in the houses
of the rich or the palaces of kings
does gratitude find her only home,
but in more lowly abodes and with
lowly folk — ay, and often at the
scant table, too — she sitteth a per-
petual guest. Was it memory?
Did the Trapper at that brief moment visit his absent friend ? Did
Wild Bill recall his wayward past ?
Were the thoughts of the woman
busy with sweet scenes of earlier
days? And did memory, by thus
reminding them of the absent and
the past, of the sweet things that
had been and were, stir within
their hearts thoughts of Him from
whom all gifts descend, and of his
blessed Son, in whose honor the
day was named ?

O memory ! thou tuneful bell
that ringeth on forever, friend at
our feasts, and friend, too, let us
call thee, at our burial, what music

can equal thine? For in thy mystic globe all tunes abide, — the birthday note for kings, the marriage peal, the funeral knell, the gleeful jingle of merry mirth, and those sweet chimes that float our thoughts, like fragrant ships upon a fragrant sea, toward heaven, — all are thine! Ring on, thou tuneful bell; ring on, while these glad ears may drink thy melody; and when thy chimes are heard by me no more, ring loud and clear above my grave that peal which echoes to the heavens, and tells the world of immortality, that they who come to mourn may check their tears, and say, " *Why do we weep? He liveth still!* " — *From* " *How John Norton kept his Christmas.*"

THE TRAPPER'S IDEA OF THE HERE—
AFTER.

HE beauty of the day be
one, and the beauty of
the night be another,
Henry. The Book says,
that in the country where the
Lord himself lives, they will need
no light of the sun, nor the moon
neither, for that matter, for He
himself giveth them light. It may
be that the Scriptur' is right; and
ef the words be writ in truth, and
there be no mistake in the calcu-
lation, I dare say it be right. But
it sartinly seems to me that it
would be a leetle dull and over-
regular like ef there shouldn't be
any day nor night, nor any mornin'
nor evenin'; fur the changes of
natur' be pleasant to look upon,

and I must say that I should be a
leetle out of reckonin' as to time
ef it wasn't fur the sun and the
moon ; and the stars be handy, too,
in their risin' and their settin' ef
ye are out on the water and have
any appintment at the camp ; and
there's another difficulty about
eatin' and sleepin' ; and how could
the meals be got onless ye had
somethin' to help ye fix the hour,
or was mighty exact in yer
habits ? "

"Some think," answered the
young man, interrupting his companion, "that there will be no eat-
ing or sleeping there ; but that
everybody will live without " —

"Henry," interrupted the Trapper in return, "Henry, ye sartinly
be too wise to believe any sech
silliness ; eatin' and sleepin' be in
the order of natur', and it's onnateral to go without 'em. The better
the place, and the happier ye be, the
more 'arnest is the appetite and the
sweeter be the sleep. The sorrow-

ful eat leetle; and them that be
grievin' know leetle of slumber.
It's sartinly foolish to suppose that
the things that be nateral to the
body here, won't be nateral to the
body there. Be I right, boy, in
this?"

"They say," responded the
young man, "that is, some say,
that in the spirit world, people
have no bodies at all."

"Henry, ye be sartinly crazy!
I mean they be crazy that talk in
that way. Bodies! How can there
be any people without bodies? And
how shall we know each other?
How be ye and me and the Lad to
consort together onless we can see
each other? and what about the
pups — yis, Henry, what about
the pups? There sartinly must be
eatin' and sleepin' ef the dogs is
to be round; and ye sartinly can't
conceit that any spot would be
homelike and rational to live in
to a man of my natur' and habits,
onless the dogs be in the cabin."

"It may be you are right, John Norton," answered the young man, smiling; "I am only telling you what some people think. I don't say they are right in their thinking. They have their ideas of heaven, and you have yours. What sort of a place do you think heaven will be, John Norton?"

"Henry," answered the Trapper, "I've thought a good deal of that; yis, I've thought a good deal of that. Ye see, I'm gittin' on in years, and, though I don't conceit I've come to the eend of the trail, yit, still I'm gittin' on that way; and, as ye have axed me the ques- tion, I'll answer it jest as I feel. I don't conceit that heaven be very onlike the 'arth. It can't be much prittier," — and the old man paused a moment, and gazed off upon the level surface of the lake, which as yet knew no ripple, for the morning wind had not begun to blow, and the great mountains were reflected in the still depths,

from base to summit; and then he
lifted his eyes till his vision commanded the eastern sky, now all
aglow with the morning light.
Long and earnestly he gazed as
one gazes at a spectacle too lovely
and majestic to be lightly admired;
and then he turned his eyes upon
his companion and said, while he
swept his hand outward with the
most natural of gestures, "Henry,
this be heaven, ef the Lad and the
pups was here and the girl was
found, and the vagabonds was
within easy range."

The young man laughed long
and heartily.

"Ye be pleased, boy," continued
the Trapper; "ye be pleased at the
conceit of an old man; and I dare
say my words seem foolish to ye;
but they be the words of my heart.
And I be glad to hear ye laugh;
for though we be on 'arnest work,
and a life be in jeopardy it may
be, yit the laugh of the innercent
never hinders their workin'. And

I say agin, ef the Lad and the pups
was here, and the girl was found,
and the vagabonds was in easy
range, and the Lord didn't inter-
fere, but let things happen as they
naterally would happen, this would
be heaven." — *From " Adirondack
Tales." Vol. ii.*

THE GAMBLER'S DEATH.

EYOND the balsam thicket the gambler made his stand. Carson, the detective, was in full pursuit, and as he burst through the balsams he found himself within twenty feet of his antagonist. Both men stood for an instant, each with a pistol in his hand, each looking full at the other. Both were experts. Each knew the other.

"You count," said the gambler coolly.

"*One, two, three,*" said the detective. "*Fire !*"

One pistol alone sounded. The gambler's had failed to explode!

"You've won, you needn't deal again," said the gambler. And

then he dropped. The red stain on his white shirt-front showed where he was hit.

"There's some lint and bandage," said the detective, and he flung a small package into the gambler's lap. "I hope you won't die, Dick Raymond."

"Oh, it was all fair, Carson," said the other carelessly. "I've held a poor hand from the start "—

He paused; for the detective had rushed on, and he was alone.

Twenty rods further on, the detective caught up with the Trapper, who was calmly recharging his piece. On the edge of the ledge above, the half-breed lay dead, the lips drawn back from his teeth, and his ugly countenance distorted with hate and rage. A rifle, whose muzzle smoked, lay at his side; and the edge of the Trapper's left ear was bleeding.

"I've shot Dick Raymond by the balsam thicket," said the detective. "I'm afraid he's hard hit."

"I'll go and see the boy," answered the Trapper. "You'll find
Henry furder up. There's only
two runnin'. You and he can
bring 'em in."

The detective disappeared like a
flash in the direction the Trapper
had pointed.

"Ah me," said the old man, "I
hope the boy isn't bad hit," and he
turned on his trail, and moved
quickly down toward the balsam
thicket.

The gambler was seated in a
reclining attitude, his body resting
on the mosses, his shoulders and
head supported by a rock, which,
covered thickly with other mosses
itself, made for his growing weakness a natural pillow. The package of lint, which the detective had
thrown to him as he dashed away,
after the fatal interview, lay within
reach unopened. Only a stain on
the white linen showed where he
was hit, for the hemorrhage was all
internal.

Through the trees, here and there, the bright water of the lake showed clearly. The little rivulet that issued from the Trapper's spring ran with tuneful gurgling through the swale, and filtered itself into the lake through sands pure as its own limpid stream. In the pines overhead were soothing noises. The young balsams yielded their gummy sweetness to the damp air. The pistol, by whose failure to explode he had escaped the crime of murder, lay by his side, while a dozen cards, that had been flung from his pocket as he dropped, were lying scattered about, — a suggestive commentary on the frivolity and sinfulness of his life. His eyes were open, gazing through the branches of the intervening trees at the bright patches of the shining water beyond, and the little rill soothed the stillness with its lapsing sound. One would hardly think that so unprincipled a life could come to its close as peacefully as the peacefulness of nature, which, because of its inanimate- ness perhaps, had committed no sin, and could therefore be dis- turbed by no remorse. But such apparently was the case ; for the look in the eyes was as placid as the lake at which they gazed, and the lines of his face were as calm and peaceful as a child's, when, just before he falls asleep, his memory is busy with the happi- ness of the day he has enjoyed, and to which, ere he sleeps, he would say a pleasant farewell.

The old Trapper saw, as he descended the hill, the body re- clining on the mosses at the edge of the balsam thicket. The earth gave back no sound as he ad- vanced, and he reached the gam- bler, and was standing almost at his very feet, ere the young man was aware of his presence ; but as the form of the Trapper passed be- tween him and the shining water, he turned his gaze up to his face, and, after studying the grave lines for a moment, said, —

"You've won the game, old man."

The Trapper for a moment made no reply. He looked steadfastly into the young man's countenance, fixed his eyes on the red stain on the left breast, and then said, —

"Shall I look at the hole, boy?"

The gambler smiled pleasantly and nodded his head, saying, "It's the natural thing to do in these cases, I believe." Lifting his hands, he unbuttoned the collar, and unscrewed the solitaire stud from the white bosom. The Trapper knelt by the young man's side, and laying back the linen from the chest, wiped with a piece of lint the blood stain from the white skin, and carefully studied the edges of the wound, seeking to ascertain the direction which the bullet had taken as it penetrated the flesh. At last he drew his face back, and lifted himself to his feet, not a shade in the expression of his face revealing his thought.

"Is it my last deal, old man?" asked the gambler carelessly.

"I have seed a good many wounds," answered the Trapper, "and I've noted the direction of a good many bullets, and I never knowed a man live who was hit where ye be hit ef the lead had the slant inward, as the piece had that has gone into ye."

For a minute the young man made no reply. No change came to his countenance. He turned his eyes from the Trapper's face, and looked pleasantly off toward the water. He even whistled softly a line or two of an old love ballad; then he paused, and, drawn perhaps by the magnetism of the steady gaze which the eyes of the Trapper fixed upon him, he looked again into the old man's face, and said, —

"What is it, John Norton?"

"I be sorry fur ye, boy," an-

swered the old man. "I be sorry
fur ye, fur life be sweet to the
young, and I wish that yer years
might be many on the arth."

"I fancy there's a good many
who will be glad to hear I'm out
of it," was the careless response.

"I don't doubt ye have yer
faults, boy," answered the Trapper, "and I dare say ye have lived
loosely, and did many deeds that
was better ondid, but the best use
of life be to learn how to live, and
I feel sartin ye'd have got better
as ye got older, and made the last
half of yer life wipe out the fust,
so that the figures fur and agin ye
would have balanced in the Jedgment."

"You aren't fool enough to believe what the hypocritical church
members talk, are you, John
Norton? You don't believe that
there's any Judgment Day, do
you?"

"I don't know much about
church members," answered the

Trapper, "fur I've never ben in the settlements ; leastwise, I've never studied the habits of the creturs, and I dare say that they differ, bein' good and bad, and I've seed some that was sartinly vagabonds. No, I don't know much about church members, but I sartinly believe ; yis, I know there be a day when the Lord shall jedge the livin' and the dead ; and the honest Trapper shall stand on one side, and the vagabond that pilfers his skins and steals his traps shall stand on the other. This is what the Book says, and it sartinly seems reasonable ; fur the deeds that be did on the arth be of two sorts, and the folks that do 'em be of two kind, and atween the two, the Lord, ef he notes anything, must make a dividin' line."

"And when do you think this judgment is, John Norton ?" asked the gambler, as if he was actually enjoying the crude but honest ideas of his companion. The Trap-

per hesitated a moment before he
spoke, then he said, —

"I conceit that the jedgment
be always goin' on. It's a court
that never adjourns, and the de-
serters and the knaves and the
disobedient in the rigiment be
always on trial. But I conceit
that there comes a day to every
man, good and bad, when the
record of his deeds be looked over
from the start, and the good and
the bad counted up; and in that
day he gits the final jedgment,
whether it be fur or agin him.
And now, boy," continued the old
man solemnly, with a touch of
infinite tenderness in the vibrations of his voice, "ye be nigh
the jedgment day, yerself, and the
deeds ye have did, both the good
and the bad, will be passed in re-
view."

"I reckon there isn't much
chance for me if your view is
sound, John Norton." And for
the first time his tone lost its
cheerful recklessness.

"The court be a court of marcy;
and the Jedge looks upon them
that comes up fur trial as ef he was
their Father."

"That ends it, old man," answered the gambler. "My father
never showed me any mercy when
I was a boy. If he had, I shouldn't
have been here now. If I did a
wrong deed, I got it to the last
inch of the lash," and the words
were more intensely bitter because
spoken so quietly.

"The fathers of the arth, boy,
be not like the Father of heaven,
for I have seen 'em correct their
children beyend reason and without marcy. They whipped in their
rage, and not in their wisdom;
they whipped because they was
strong, and not because of their
love; they whipped when they
should have forgiven, and got what
they 'arnt — the hatred of their
children. But the Father of
heaven be different, boy. He
knows that men be weak, as well

as wicked. He knows that half of 'em haven't had a fair chance, and so he overlooks much ; and when he can't overlook it, I conceit he sorter forgives in a lump. Yis, he subtracts all he can from the evil we have did, boy, and ef that isn't enough to satisfy his feelin's toward a man that might have ben different, ef he'd had a fair start, he jest wipes the whole row of figurs clean out at the askin'."

"At the asking?" said the gambler ; "that's a mighty quick deal. Did you ever pray, John Norton?"

"Sartin, sartin, I be a prayin' man," said the Trapper sturdily.

"At the asking!" murmured the gambler softly.

"Sartin, boy," answered the Trapper, "that's the line the trail takes, ye can depend on it ; and it will bring ye to the eend of the Great Clearin' in peace."

"It's a quick deal," said the gambler, speaking to himself, utterly

unconscious of the incongruity of
his speech to his thought. " It's a
quick deal, but I can see that it
might end as he says, if the feeling
was right."

For a moment nothing was said.
The Trapper stood looking steadfastly at the young man on the
moss, as he lay with his quiet
clean-cut face turned up to the
sky, to whose color had already
come the first shade of the awful
whiteness.

Up the mountain a rifle cracked.
Neither stirred. A red squirrel
ran out upon the limb, twenty
feet above the gambler's head, and
shook the silence into fragments
with his chattering ; then sat gazing with startled eyes at the two
men underneath.

" Can you pray, old man ? "
asked the gambler quietly.

" Sartinly," answered the Trapper.

" Can you pray in words ? "
asked the gambler again,

For a moment the Trapper hesitated. Then he said, —

"I can't say that I can. No, I sartinly can't say that I could undertake it with a reasonable chance of gittin' through; leastwise, it wouldn't be in a way to help a man any."

"Is there any way, old man, in which we can go partners?" asked the gambler, the vocabulary of whose profession still clung to him in the solemn counselling.

"I was thinkin' of that," answered the Trapper; "yis, I was thinkin' ef we couldn't sorter jine works, and each help the other by doin' his own part himself. Yis," continued the old man, after a moment's reflection, "the plan's a good 'un — ye pray fur yerself, and I'll pray fur myself — and ef I can git in anything that seems likely to do ye sarvice, ye can count on it, as ye can on a grooved barrel.

"And now, boy," said the Trap-

per, with a sweetly solemn enthu-
siasm, such as faith might give
to a supplicating saint, — which
lighted his features until his countenance fairly shone with a light
which came out of it from a
radiance within, rather than upon
it from the sun overhead — "now,
boy, remember that the Lord is
Lord of the woods as well as of
the cities, and that he heareth the
prayin' of the poor hunter under
the pines, as well as the great
preachers in the pulpits, and that
when sins be heavy, and death be
nigh, His ear and His heart be
both open.   There was no use of
His Son's dyin' ef the Father can't
be forgivin'."

The Trapper knelt on the moss
at the gambler's feet.   He clasped
the fingers of his great hands until
they interlaced, and lifted his wrin-
kled face upward.   He said not a
word ; but an Eye that was watching noted that the strongly chiselled lips, seamed with age, moved

and twitched now and then, and
the same Eye saw, as the silent
prayer went on, two great tears
leave the protection of the closed
lids, and roll down the rugged
cheek. The gambler also closed
his eyes ; then his hands quietly
stole one into the other, and, avoid-
ing the bloody stain, rested on his
breast ; and thus, the old man who
had lived beyond the limit of man's
days, and the young one, cut down
at the threshold of mature life —
the one kneeling on the mosses,
with his face lifted to heaven, the
other lying on the mosses, with his
face turned toward the same sky,
without word or uttered speech, —
prayed to the Divine mercy which
beyond the heaven and the sky saw
the two men underneath the pines,
and met, we may not doubt, with
needed answer the silent up-going
prayer.

The two opened their eyes
nearly at the same instant. They
looked for a moment at each other,

and then the gambler feebly lifted his hand, and put it into the broad palm of the Trapper. Not a word was said. No word was needed. Sometimes men understand each other better than by talking. Then the gambler picked the diamond stud from the spot where it rested, slipped the solitaire from his finger, and said, as he handed them to the Trapper, —

"There's a girl in Montreal that will like these. You will find her picture inside my vest, when you bury me. Her address is inside the picture case. You will take them to her, John Norton?"

"She shall have them from my own hand," answered the Trapper gravely.

"You needn't disturb the picture, John Norton," said the gambler; "it's just as well, perhaps, to let it lie where it is; it's been there eight years. You understand what I mean, old man?"

"I understand," answered the

Trapper solemnly; "the pictur'
shall stay where it is."

"The pistols," resumed the gambler, and he glanced at the one
lying on the moss, "I give to you.
You'll find them true.   You will
accept them?"

The Trapper bowed his head.
It is doubtful if he could speak.
For several minutes there was
silence.   The end was evidently
nigh.   The Trapper took the gambler's hand, as if it had been the
hand of his own boy.   Indeed, perhaps the young man had found his
father at last; for surely it isn't
flesh that makes fatherhood.   Once
the young man moved as if he
would rise.   Had he been able he
would have died with his arms
round the old man's neck.   As it
was, the strength was unequal to
the impulse.   He lifted his eyes to
the old man's face lovingly, moved
his body as if he would get a little
nearer, and, as a child might speak
a loving thought aloud, said, "I am

glad I met you, John Norton," and
with the saying of the sweet words
he died.

But the water gleamed as
brightly through the trees as before ; the little rivulet sang as
tunefully ; the balsams poured
their odors forth with undimin-
ished measure, and the squirrel
crept with new courage from his
hiding-place, and, scampering out
to the limit of the branch, poured
his merry chatterings forth upon
the quiet air. The Trapper lifted
the body of the gambler in his
arms and bore him to his own
cabin, and laid him on his own
bed ; then, closing the door of the
cabin, he went to the bank that
overlooked the lake, and sounded
the two signals for the return. —
From " Adirondack Tales." Vol. ii.

THE GREAT NATIONAL PARK.

F the reader will take a map of the country, and, beginning at Niagara Falls, draw a line eastward to Mount Desert, and, with this as the central line, construct a parallelogram, he will have embraced within it such a grouping of natural scenery both as regards sublimity and beauty, along with such a multitude of resources for human recreation and entertainment, as may not be found elsewhere in connection, either on this continent or in Europe. In Niagara he beholds a world-renowned marvel. To it there is, among waterfalls, no rival on the globe. It is a majestic appearance of nature. In its awful exhibition, majesty

and sublimity reveal their highest expression. In its contemplation the beholder enjoys an experience which can never be repeated. He sees, he feels, and out of that seeing and feeling there grows up and with him remains forever a magnificent memory. Niagara is at once the sublimest of spectacles and the most impressive of recollections.

Northward of the great cataract flows the St. Lawrence : a river which surpasses all others in the world in the mystery of its origin,[1] the length and number of its tributaries, the enormous amount of water it delivers to the ocean, the

[1] The Five Great Lakes which make the St. Lawrence a geographical wonder are themselves a mystery. Geology cannot explain them. Even that stupendous Guess known as the Glacial Theory loses its audacity in the presence of these phenomena. Even its imagination, which soars like the frigate bird above human knowledge and never touches earth, tumbles ignominiously to the ground as it comes to these inland oceans, and confesses it is unable to suggest the cause of these stupendous excavations at the level centre of the continent.

evenness of its flow,[1] the multitude
of its rapids and islands, the varied
loveliness of its riparian scenery,
and the dim traditions and historic
memories which haunt, like summer reflections of night and day,
its glassy stream.

Thirty years ago the Thousand
Islands were scarcely known to the
American public. To-day they are
noted from one end of the country
to the other. The charm of their
tranquil loveliness is as delightful
to the mind as the spectacle of
Niagara is appalling. The poet
and scholar, the artist and philos-
opher, the weary business man and
college student, the angler and
tourist, — that hiveless bee that
buzzes from flower to flower and
gathers sweetness only for his own
transient entertainment, — wealth,
fashion, and fame, all resort to this
picturesque section of the noble
river, as fairies of every order are

[1] It is said that the St. Lawrence does not
change its level eight inches the whole year round.

said in elfin lore to gather once
each year at the most lovely centre
of fairyland. If our Eastern country had no other attractions for the
tourist and lover of nature than
Niagara and the Thousand Islands,
these alone would make it famous,
and draw from the South and West
thousands upon thousands of visitors each year.

But what may we say of the
Adirondacks, that Venice of the
woods whose highways are rivers,
whose paths are streams, and whose
carriages are boats? Thirty years
ago they were a wilderness, a wild,
unvalued section of the Empire
State, unknown and unnoted save
to a few sportsmen and their
guides. Suddenly they were revealed. A little volume was published which told of their extent,
their charming characteristics,
their sanitarian qualities, and their
provisions for sport. The great,
ignorant, stay-at-home, egotistic
world laughed and jeered and tried

to roar the book down. They called it a fraud and a hoax. The pictorials of the day blazoned their broadsides with caricatures of "Murray and his fools." Innumerable articles were written to the press, and editorials published, denying that there was any such extent of woods in the State, any such number of lakes, any such phenomenal connection of waterways, any such possibilities of pleasure and health as the little book portrayed. It should be remembered that there were then no hotels in the woods, no railroad facilities of entrance and exit, no accommodation for sick or well, no moneyed interest, as there is today to assist the influence of that first publication. But the facts of geography and the truth of nature were in it, and it successfully breasted the current of adverse criticism and hostile comment, of innuendo and jeer, and carried the fame of the woods over the conti-

nent ; and to-day there is no spot
betwixt the two oceans or the two
gulfs better known or more loved
by those who visit them than the
far-famed Adirondacks.

Many years have passed since I
visited them. And since I kindled
my last camp-fire on the Raquette,
I have lighted many in many places,
and as widely apart as the continent would allow. And I can well
imagine that many changes have
come to the woods whose quietude
and loneliness and the absence of
the coming and going of men made
them so attractive to me when, in
other years, I visited them. They
even say that the little wild island
I loved in the Raquette, and on
whose ledge of rock, under un-
touched trees, I built my lodge,
has been civilized by the axe and
the plough, and that the divine
silence of the Sabbath air is jarred
into discord by the clang and rattle
of a chapel bell ! But, in spite of
all these sad changes and profana-

tions, I doubt not that the woods still have their beauty, the mountains keep their majesties, the lakes glass storm and shine by day and the stars at night, and that the pools are as clear and cool as of yore, albeit they lack the flash and gleam of finny splendor which shot them through and through with color in the days when I checked their smooth surface with my trailing flies.

Yes, the woods are still there, the mountains abide, the lakes murmur converse to the shores, the rivers flow on, the pools still go round, and the trees in the warm nights drop their odorous gums to the scented mould, as they did when I saw and heard and breathed their beauty and perfume. And while these remain, the Adirondack wilderness must ever be what it is to-day, the most unique, picturesque, charming, and healthful section of the continent; the one place for all to visit, and which not

to have seen is to remain untrav-
elled.

But what shall we say of the
Horicon,[1] of Au Sable Chasm, of
the springs of Saratoga, of the
valley of the Le Moile, of the
Green Mountains, whose ridges
should be white with hotels, of the
Upper Connecticut and Winnepesaukee, of the White Mountains,
of which no one has written fit-
tingly since that priest of God and
of nature both, Starr King, died?
For the eye that sees not only the
outward form but the inner spirit
which the form conceals from most;
the ear that hears not only the
undulating sound which strikes all
ears alike, but the voice which

[1] I do not insist on this name, but I do insist
that the name of the coarse, stupid Hanoverian
King of England shall not be used to designate
this most wild and impressive of American lakes.
Lac St. Sacrement is not appropriate; Lake
George is a vulgarization; and, if it cannot be known
as Lac aux Iroquois — Lake of the Iroquois — which
is doubtless its truest name, then I prefer the name
that Cooper used to designate it, — the Horicon —
Silvery Water.

dwells within the sound and is alone
worth hearing because it alone
signalizes it with meaning ; the
nose which distinguishes between
the breaths it draws, divides common from uncommon air, and calls
that only worthy of praise that is
distinguished with some fine quality ; a choice perfume, a rare fra-
grance, a pungent trace of ozone, —
that unembodied vitalness breathed
into lower atmospheres out of
God's ; — he who has not these and
other rare gifts is not fitted to
write of woods and waters, of lakes
and mountains, of day and night, as
they come from and go into eternity, because he cannot sense their
high significance or materialize
their fine, volatile qualities into the
solid, opaque characters of human
language. These gifts King had,
and, had he lived, he would have
interpreted the White Hills as they
deserve. But, alas, he died, killed,
as was the poet White, by the fer-
vid zeal of his own genius ; and

the famous mountains remain without a prophet until this day.

Within this parallelogram, more-
over, are the Rangeley Lakes, and
Moosehead ; Bar Harbor and
Mount Desert, and Poland Springs ;
and nigh to its southern line are
the beaches of New Hampshire
and Massachusetts, Lexington and
Bunker Hill. And fringing the
eastern end of it are the caribou
and moose regions of northern
Maine and New Brunswick, the
salmon rivers that are to anglers
as the magnet is to grains of steel,
and but a little way beyond lie the
peaceful meadows of Acadia, and
the home of Evangeline.

Now at the centre of this mar-
vellous parallelogram, crowded as
it is with wonders of nature, with
every class of scenery known to
mountains and forests, rivers and
lakes, and provided with every
provision for sport and recreation,
pleasure and health, which the
enterprise and money of men can

provide, is located Lake Champlain, in many respects the most inter-esting and attractive section of the whole. It is characterized by the length and breadth of its waters ; the multitude and loveliness of its islands ; the majesty of its sur-rounding mountains ; the pastoral beauty of its shores, and the his-toric memories with which it is and must ever remain in vital and vivid connection.

For the lover of aboriginal tradi-tions and relics it supplies a field absolutely unexplored. To the angler it gives a habitat of the black bass as abundantly stocked as any other stretch of American water. To the yachtsman it affords opportunities of pleasure, navigation, and amateur seaman-ship as ample as sound or ocean coast supply, while to the canoeist and campist it extends, in its bays and rivers, its islands and its shores, its golden beaches and bold promontories, ideal condi-

tions of recreation and enjoyment, and the health which comes
to those who love the out-door life
and world.

Nor is it less remarkable for its
connections. The Adirondacks
come to its western beach, and
the Green Mountains slope grad-
ually down to its eastern shore.
The chasm of the Au Sable is
within easy walk of it, and the
Horicon is its nigh neighbor. The
ruins of Ticonderoga and Crown
Point are on it, and the delights of
the Hudson within a few hours'
travel, while by its outlet to the
north the steam-launch and sailing-
yacht can glide downward to the
broad St. Lawrence, and thence
go upward to the Thousand
Islands or downward to Quebec,
Montmorency, and the Saguenay.
Its waters are traversed by steamers that, in size and appointments,
are excelled only by the floating
palaces of Long Island Sound,
and the railways that touch it at

many points enable the tourist to pass, by day or night, in any direction. Intelligently estimated, and weighed in the balance of considerate comparison, it is the most beautiful lake on the continent, and to him who sees it for the first time it is both a revelation and an education.

Congress may resolve and newspaper correspondents may with hasty pen declare that this or that spot, distinguished by some local phenomena, shall be known as the National Park, but neither formal resolution nor hasty verdict of casual writers can change the geography of the continent or the facts of nature ; and these declare — and with an emphasis that cannot be misunderstood or unheeded by the intelligent — that the *Great National Park for the whole American people* lies within the lines of the parallelogram I have suggested, and to it there is not now, and never can be, on the continent, a rival. Niagara, the Thousand Islands, the Adirondacks, the Horicon, Champlain with its battle memories, the White Mountains, and the coast of Maine are all in it, and there they will remain forever. These great and admirable objects of nature can never be removed either to the south or west, but will abide where God has placed them; and to them, to see, to admire, to marvel, and enjoy, will the thousands and millions of the American people who love nature and have reverence for shrines annually journey.

It was on the shores of the Atlantic that the Republic was born. Here was she cradled, and here was her early loveliness grown. The American people know this fact, and to the East will the millions continue to come as to the birthplace of the nation. The continental lines of travel will cross the continent from ocean to ocean, not from gulf to gulf, and the millions upon millions that are in the years to come to people the prairies and valleys of the Great West will seek recreation and pleasure among the hills and lakes, the rivers and mountains, of the section I have suggested, and which is, by nature and fact, and is destined to to be called, *The Great National Park of the Republic.*

If those who now control the present lines of travel, and who, with their successors, should naturally construct the additional accommodations as called for, are wise, they will do well to bear in mind that the places the people want to see are here in the East, and that the great bulk of the people who would fain see them are in the West. The places are here, the people are there, and how to bring people and places together easily and quickly is the problem for them to solve. The pleasure resorts of which we have spoken find their patrons to-day chiefly from the cities of the Atlantic Coast. But the population east of the Alleghanies and the Great Lakes is but a small fraction of the mighty total which represents the nation. The sceptre of numbers has already passed to the prairies, and the sceptre of wealth is sure to follow. But what are these compared with those great centres of population which will be grouped here and there clean across the great basin which extends westward to the Rocky Mountains? It is not beyond reason to believe that at least one of those Western cities will have, within fifty years, more inhabitants than Philadelphia, New York, and Boston combined. If the causes which have given London its five millions are not so exceptional as never to be operant again or elsewhere, then is it as certain as the sun shines that Chicago, at some period not re-

mote, will have within her corpo-
rate limits from ten to fifteen
millions of people.

If the Republic endures in peace
and prosperity, there surely will be
gathered within two centuries on
the shore of Lake Michigan a city
which for the wealth and number
of its citizens, the magnificence of
its appearance, and the power of
the forces it represents, has never
been equalled since men were
grouped into nations, felt the force
of centralization, and built cities
to express the grandeur of their
ambitions and the glory of their
civilization.

The old New-England nests are
empty and cold because the young
birds which once filled and warmed
them with life have flown abroad.
With their wings came longings,
and singly and in flocks they went
forth to find new places for new
nests and new colonies. But the
lines of their flight were not hidden, and the world knows whither

they went and where they are. But with them went love for the old places and memory; and the sons and daughters of New England remember her mountains and her lakes, her rivers and her shores, and the homes of their fathers. Nor will they ever forget her hilltops and her valleys. These and their descendants still see the stars of the East and love them, and while blood is thicker than water and prosperity abides with the nation, a long and ever-growing procession of men and women, half pilgrims and half tourists, will with the coming of summer and autumn journey eastward to see the fields and woods, the lakes and hills that their forefathers saw, and rekindle the torch of family affection at the hearthstones of their ancestors. The West and the East of the nation stand connected as children are connected with parents and midday is related to morning.

I foresee the day, not as remote,
but nigh, when the Great Lakes
shall be utilized for the purposes
of pleasure as fully as for traffic ;
when magnificent steamers shall
take the summer tourists at
Chicago wharves and transport
them eastward ; when the Thousand Islands and Niagara shall be
in direct water connection for
excursionists from the West ;
when long trains of palace cars
shall run direct, without change,
from Chicago, St. Louis, Minne-
apolis, and Denver to the Adirondacks, Lake Champlain, and the
White Mountains ; the lovely
Winnepesaukee, the lakes of
Maine and its celebrated beaches ;
when the great pleasure resorts of
the nation, which are here and ever
will remain here in the East, will
be in as direct and facile connection with the cities of the West as
are Philadelphia, New York, and
Boston to-day ; and I anticipate
that this annual visitation of thou-

sands from the West to the East,
as prompted by the love of pleasure, of health, and ancestral memories, will not be the least among
those unifying forces upon which
we must rely to preserve the great
Republic, as its millions multiply,
in the unity which is born from
and maintained by mutual ac-
quaintance and affection between
its widely separated sections. —
*From "Lake Champlain and its
Shores."*

ND now, dear friends, known and unknown — for if you but love the out-door life as I do love it, you are friends to me, even kith and kin, by a relationship finer and closer than that of blood — likeness of nature; I commend you to the woods and waters, as to the Grace of God found in them by those who may receive it. May rest, health, and peace come to you as you enter them and remain. May you grow in grace of nature, as you do in knowledge of her as you likely will — for there is that in nature which maketh all who truly love her like herself; and something of her calm stillness, her starry expanses, her graceful

suavities, and that sweet expect-
ancy which waits on fair sunsets
forecasting fair to-morrows, come
to us who love her as we age.

In bringing this, the last of our
gathered cones to our camp-fire, I
do recall a little book sent out long
years ago, which told my country-
men of the woods and waters of
the Adirondacks.   I do not remember how long ago it was ; nor do I
wish to.   I count the years ahead
and forget the years behind.   I
know no higher wisdom.   My
past is as a little space.   My future
has boundless horizons and endless
perspectives in it.   Of these the
woods tell, for

He who sleeps in woods has time to think.

And out of leisurely thought
springs firmest faith.

Here, then, is to our meeting
under trees ; on golden stretch of
river ; at foot of rapids, safely run ;
on portage, laughing under heavy
burdens ; at the pool's edge, when

the rod bends ; by camp-fires' light, and at the courteous table in that hall whose walls no hand may touch and whose roof is hung with stars. I lift this cup of clean, cool water, dipped from the brook that rippling runs beside my camp, and drain it to our happy meeting where

> " Good digestion waits on appetite, and health on both."

W. H. H. MURRAY.